THE HORDES
DOUGLAS OWEN

THE HORDES
DOUGLAS OWEN

WICKED TALES

https://wickedtales.ca
An imprint of DAOwen Publications

The Hordes / Douglas Owen
Edited by MJ Moores

ISBN 978-1-928094-33-3
EISBN 978-1-928094-34-0

Jacket art: MMT Productions

10 9 8 7 6 5 4 3 2 1

Chapters

About the Author

To Sheila, for letting me express my muse

A Hot Day

The traffic stretches from Whitby as far as I can see. A quick glance at the dash shows the time as 30 minutes past when my ass should be sitting at my desk. Shit's going to hit the fan on this one. If the sun would only stop killing us this summer we might be able to survive.

It's July 3rd, and yesterday saw a record temperature – just over 43 °C or a little cooler than hell. Sitting in traffic on the highway puts everyone at egg-frying temp. I play with the air conditioning, hoping it can keep up with the demand. Just one more summer, that's all I need the Focus to last.

Three cars are on the shoulder. Blue, black, and silver. I keep my attention on the road, not looking at the argument or the one passenger grasping at the others through an open window. In this heat, who would keep their window open anyway?

The check engine light flashes on then off. The motor's fan starts to whine and a quick glance at the temp brings out a sigh. Almost all the way into the red. Great. Another shitty day, and now I'll cook even more. I turn off the air, push the heater all the way to "Kill me now," and flip it on. The lava pours out and I roll down a window. This is really going to suck ass. What a great way to start a Monday. How much shittier can 2023 get?

It takes two hours to get just past Pickering. Normally, I would fly through in under twenty minutes. Three more cars sit on the shoulder of the highway with steam coming from under their hoods and, as I pass them, the road opens up. The dashboard clock reads out 9:37 as the green glow fights to escape the glare. So much for being early.

I pull off the highway at Markham Road and battle my way to the college. A few minutes later and the Focus sits in my parking space, engine not stopping even though I've removed the key. For a few seconds it chugs, sputters, refuses to give up life, then it's as quiet as can be. Sweat stains cover me from collar to socks. I'm not worried. No, I have another change of clothes sitting in my office. The idea of cool air conditioning floats through my over-heated mind. This is a great day to take advantage of being the IT manager.

The college employs multiple chillers and redundant power supplies for our computer room – thank God. Nothing beats the heat and humidity more than the good old fashion need to keep the systems running. It takes only a few minutes for me to make my way into the secured room and sit down, undo my shirt another button, and pulled off smelly shoes.

Racks and racks of servers blink green and yellow lights between me and the outside world. This is my safe place. So I pull out the bag containing my "EMERGENCY" clothes, kept stored in the bottom drawer, and change. One of the more interesting things about IT people is we find everything useful. From small throw-away hand towels to big boxes, we find a use for everything. I clean up and look better than if traffic had moved quickly.

Once clean, there's little to do but sit back and wait for something to happen, or the end of the day, whichever comes first. Usually the shifts are uneventful. The odd ping from a server in Turkey or something. Nothing we can't handle.

But the lights go out.

Emergency floodlights switch on. A red glow fills the server room as I pull on my pants. Only one monitor works during brownouts, so I walk over to it and query the system with a few key strokes.

Nothing.

This shouldn't happen. Even if everything is down, there must be a return of how the generators are doing. I type the command again to query the system on the power status. Nothing but a blank screen and blinking curser responds.

Not wanting to show the definition of insanity, I grab my shoes and head to the door. Times like these, the chillers go to half-power.

Operating procedure says to monitor the temp outside the room and open the doors if it is cooler outside than in, stationing a fan for air flow. So I go to the door, stare at the thermostat outside and compared it to the one inside the door. I will the one at the door to stay down.

It takes 23 minutes for the first backup power supply to start beeping. Not a nice light beep, but a throaty nagging mother-in-law one. I check it out and decide to turn the alarm off. Nothing I can do in here and the system it controls is redundant.

Something bangs against the door. I spin around and hurry toward it. This time of year usually sees very few people on campus, so how would someone know I'm in here? Curiosity forces me to investigate. The noise becomes furious with the sound of a slapping hand against glass.

When I come out from behind one of the server racks, standing at the door, eyes wide, stands a small Asian girl. Her long hair appears wild from wind and she's sweating, but that could be from the heat. One hand bangs against the thick, reinforced window while the other turns the handle frantically. I read her shirt while walking to the door, trying to make it appears as if I'm not staring at her breasts. "Asian Smart". At least it gets a giggle from me.

I hit the intercom. "Yes?"

Nothing. I can hear muffled yelling but can't make out what she's saying.

Once again I hit the intercom. "You have to press the button." I point to the side of the door.

Her hand slams against the intercom. "Help! Let me in! They're coming!" Her voice holds no accent and the shrill sound grates against my already raw nerves.

"I'm not allowed to. If you want, the nurse is also on emergency power and she can…" Her gaze moves to the right and I follow it. Hell walks toward her. Not really hell, but something that probably crawled out of it just a few minutes ago.

Jesus, one of the grounds keepers I used to smoke with, walks toward the girl, about twenty paces away. *Walks* is a strong word. Lumbers is better. His black hair hangs loose just like the arms on either side of his body. A long gash down the side of one cheek ends just before his wide open jaw. No blood drops from the wound and his milky eyes only stare straight ahead.

3

DOUGLAS OWEN

I open the door, pull the girl inside, and slam it shut. She hugs me. Frantic sounds come from her mouth but she speaks so fast I can hardly make anything out. Probably because nothing separates her words as she speaks. I just stare at the door as Jesses bumps up against it.

"Holly fuck!" I hit the intercom. "Are you okay, Jesses?"

As if to answer me, Jesses bumps his head against the glass and tries to walk through the door. If it wasn't for the heat emanating from the girl's body, I might forget about her. No, probably not. The scent of musk along with fresh sweat cloaks her. If I could smell fear, she'd reek of it.

"He's dead," she says, staring at the door. "Oh God, oh God, oh God." She finally lets go of me. "What the fuck have I done!" Her hand rises as she lowers her face. "It's all my fault!"

"What?" Yeah, I've had great aspirations about getting an Asian girl into the server room — a geeky one who'd really appreciate the pure power of all the processors in here. Now, with one basically melting before me, I really turn on my inner Einstein.

She grabs handfuls of her hair. "I killed him."

"I'm sure that's not true." I gesture to the door. "He's there, still walking about."

"You don't understand." She breathes in a shuddering breath. "I pulled into a parking space. Turned up the stereo. My foot came off the break and hit the gas." She points to Jesses. "He flew back from the curb. That gash... I did that." Tears build in her eyes. "I checked him and there was no pulse, no breathing, no heartbeat. I called 911 and cops were on their way. I waited as all his blood spilled out and he died!"

I stare, mouth agape, watching this small girl explain how Jesses, who bangs on the door now, died just outside. A deep breath rattles into my lungs and I shake my head. "You probably just dazed him or something." Taking her hand, I approach the door and hit the intercom. "Jesses, are you okay buddy?"

I can just make out moaning from the other side.

"He's fucking dead!" Her voice approaches shrill as she sinks to the floor.

I catch more movement in the background. A few other people mill about, and another person, with what appears to be bullet holes in his

4

torso, approaches. I recognize him as Dr. Harper, a middle aged man who teaches molecular chemistry. His lab coat is a muddled red instead of the pristine white he loves, only rivaled by the jaundice pallor of his complexion. As he stumbles forward, he drops a severed arm and opens a blood stained mouth. Cloudy eyes stare at me as he bumps into the glass door.

"Shit." I show my waning intelligence once more, but the point comes across.

My guest sobs on the floor. I only wanted to spend the day surfing the net and watching videos, but it seems the whole world has gone to hell.

Without thinking much about it, I help the girl to her feet and lead her deep into the server room. We walk with a quick pace, past racks and air vents blowing somewhat cool air.

The ground shakes and a muffled explosion rumbles through the air.

"What the fuck was that?" she cries out.

I stop, pull her around to face me. "You need to calm down or we'll get stuck in here. Understand?"

She nods.

"Good." I glance about. "What's your name?"

"Ming, but everyone calls me Mindy." She sniffs. A tear runs down her cheek.

"Okay, Mindy it is. I'm Steve." I hold out my hand. "Glad to meet you."

She takes my hand and gives a little squeeze. I guess something tells girls to trust me. It's the big brother syndrome and why I'm still single.

I lead her to the emergency exit, but stop. The glass brick wall shows a bunch of shapes lumbering around or just standing there. Something warns me to check first.

With a quick glance, I find a server keyboard and monitor, pull them out, and hit a few commands. Soon, there's a window on the screen showing the security camera feed from the hallway. My eyebrows raise, they're still running, and a smile twinges at the corners of my mouth. In the hallway is a scene from Dante's. Three bodies are on the ground and a number of people rip away at the flesh. After seeing Dr. Harper's snack, there's no way I'm going out there.

"We're trapped," Mindy says.

"You're never truly trapped." I scan the cameras, check for any

5

escape. "The lab."

"The what?"

I tap the monitor. "The lab. Twenty metres that way." With one finger, I point to the south wall. "We can lift the raised floor and get into it."

"And what? Wait?"

"No, not that bad." I take her hand and head to the south wall. "Once we're in there, the emergency door opens to the outside. My car is parked nearby. Do you have a cell phone?"

"Duh, of course." A little ting of *are you for real* enters her voice. She pulls out one of those huge phones all the teens and under twenties are using. "Network is down."

"No signal? How about data?"

She taps a few times. "Nope, nothing."

I pull mine out, not even wondering if it works or not. "Same here." With a swipe I change it to the college network. "Internal's up."

She shakes her head. "Not for me."

"Faculty," I say, as if that explains why, and it does. The look in her eyes says she pieces it together, like most do, that there are two signals in the college: one for students and a secured one for the faculty to use. I connect to the servers, wait for the prompt, and entered my password. A terminal will allow me to up the access, but have to do it before leaving the room. "One sec." I scurry to a terminal, pull up the user profiles, and advance my access to a domain admin. "There."

Mindy stares at me. "What now?"

I lift four floor boards to reveal the main. Cables run toward the south lab. My plan is to follow them and get into the south lab without actually entering the halls.

"I thought these walls were fire breaks," Mindy says.

"Everyone does." I hold out my hand. "After you."

There's only two feet of clearance between the main and raised floor. Each square is about two feet across, or just enough room for a small person to crawl through. I'm not small.

Mindy squeezes past wires and cables in the small space with no issues. I follow her, my back rubbing against the same space every inch. I enjoy the view while the light lasts. But once past a certain point it becomes harder to see, and her firm backside is a blur in the limited light.

Mindy pulls out her cell and uses the flashlight app to see. I motion to follow the cables, indicating where they lead up through the raised floor, and the only other source of light. They would be out of the way of windows and doors. Dust covers a lot of the surface, and once again happiness for no allergies dances in my mind.

As I pass the break area of the main server room, the sound of dragging feet echoes around us. Fists pound against the floor, trying to get through, but soon the noise retreats as we grow closer to our goal. I can imagine the bodies above clambering to get at us. Fingers searching for flesh. No one has ever told me my imagination needs work.

Scraping happens just before I reach the lab break-wall and I swear something on the other side of the floor sniffs. To her credit, Mindy just keeps crawling.

When we attain the main optical lines coming into the lab, I push an access tile aside. Something pushes it back.

Mindy's lips part, but I put a finger against them, feeling the softness. She closes her mouth. I push the tile up and aside again, and as it comes back, I push against it again.

"No fucking way," whispers a deep, harsh voice.

"Frank?" I whisper back. "Frank, it's Steve. I have someone with me. Stop putting the tile back."

The pressure comes off the tile and I push it aside along with a few others. Mindy crawls up first and I follow. Frank just stands there staring at her.

My friend and fellow tech support worker can out stare anyone. His huge bug-eyes stand out in contrast to nothing else about his big body. A broad, flat nose and puffy lips lay on a wide face and even wider neck. Not that he holds a lot of muscle. On the contrary, Frank's body mass make him hard to miss, just like the side of a barn. The college even bought a special chair for him. I'm still shocked I was able to hold the tile back knowing he placed his weight against it.

"Jesus, Steve, you scared the life out of me." He pats his arm with a hand. "Who's the girl?"

"Mindy." She steps back from his leering gaze. "And I'm not a girl."

"Sorry, no offense." Like most of us, Frank pulls back from the starship-like defence Mindy verbally puts up. He cradles an arm and glances about nervously. "Can you give me a hand, Steve?"

"Sure, what's up?" I glance at his arm.

"One of those freaks bit into me before I knew what was going on." He pulls away a hand from the arm and a bandage shows against his dark skin. "Thing broke the skin but little else. Punched the guy and he let go. Stings like a mother!" With exaggerated care, he pulls away the bandage. "Can't get the bitch to stop bleeding."

I guide him to a chair. "Let me get a good look at it."

He sits, causing the chair to squeak out a complaint. The wound doesn't look that bad, but the skin around it already shows puffiness. Swelling is never a good thing. I touch part of it and a green puss dribbles out. Infection? But even though Frank grossly outweighs most people, he never smells of stink. Even his breath, which most people ignore, does not offend. It's one of the reasons why we're friends. That and he's the only one I don't have to watch when he rolls dice during a game of D&D.

"It's not that bad," I say to him.

"Oh, come on. I know what bad looks like and I'm sure green isn't supposed to come out of me from the arm."

Mindy looks around my side. "Didn't you guys take first aid or something? I thought all faculty had to be certified."

Frank Points to it without lifting his head. "Only if you have exposure to the students. Other than that, we can maybe put on a bandage without cutting ourselves. Probably, that is."

Mindy grabs the kit off the wall. "Great. Two geeks and no nurse." She picks up a bandage and a small bottle of peroxide, then helps clean the wound. "Guess I'll just have to rely on what Mom taught me."

Mindy does a good job with the wound. She cleans it up but uses the last of the peroxide on it. Must sting for Frank, who shows great restraint, flinching little. Man it bubbles and fizzes. The green stuff starts weeping again but a couple of gauzes later and Frank can stop holding the arm. She steps back and admires her work.

"Mom would have put an ointment on it or something. Since we don't have anything like that, just cleaning it will have to do." Mindy squeezes his arm. "You'll be okay."

"Thanks," Frank says. I swear he's blushing, but sometimes you just can't tell.

"Are you feeling okay?" Mindy stares up at Frank, her hand lingering on his pudgy arm.

"Yeah, just a little chill." Frank crosses his arms with a shiver. "We keep these rooms so cold."

Mindy glances down, takes her hand away from his arm and crosses hers. "Maybe we should get out of here?"

Both turn toward me. Why, I don't know. Frank maybe thinks I'm senior to him, but really, we were hired on the same day. Mindy could be looking toward me for guidance, knowing she's a lot younger than I am. Not by much, probably, but yes, a little.

"We could make it to my place. At least it's out of the city." I scratch my head. "Not sure how well my car will perform, and Mindy's is out front and in a little bit of a wreck." Frank smiles and I know what's going through his head about the girl. "What about your car, Frank?"

"I rode my bike today." He glances down at his arm. "Guess that's not happening this afternoon."

"Well, my car it is." I stare at Frank. "Which way to the emergency exit?"

Muggy and Hot

Mindy and Frank just keep staring at me, as if I'm supposed to know what to do. I'm blank. Not a thought in the world. First apocalypse for me, so how should I know what to do? So, I stand.

"Which way, Frank?"

He snaps out of whatever thing his mind is busy contemplating and points to the wall behind me. "Just down the line of servers there." He drops his arm and looks toward Mindy. "How good are you at heights?"

Mindy tilts her head a little. "Good, why?"

"The stairs are down."

I stop half way to the door. "What?"

"The stairs are down," Frank calls out to me.

I glance back. "Those things are attracted to sound."

"Fuck," Frank says. "No wonder they kept coming at the doors and wall."

I stop and face him. "What? Why?"

"They don't flinch when you bang on stuff." He shrugs. "Most things run from banging."

Mindy tugs at Frank's arm. "What'd you mean the stairs are down?"

"It means they're down. What else?"

"The pull part is down?"

"No, the stairs are down," Frank says.

I reach the door and glance at the sign about the alarm going off if opened. Well, nothing to do but try it. A push against the bar and the door opens. I look down.

The absence of the alarm unnerves me, but only for a second. What causes me to whirl is the empty air my foot hovers over. Frank told the truth, the stairs lay in a wreck of twisted metal on the ground. I count ten bodies struggling in the mess of metal, pieces of brown rebar or rot iron sticking out of them. Their hands grasp at the air, heads twisting about, milky eyes searching. A few heads turn toward the door and my hovering foot. Several lumbering bodies cross the small back parking lot and head to the now open door. Vacant eyes fix on me. Icy fingers dance on my spine.

I search the area, not missing anything — even the backed-up traffic on the highway — then close the door, and sink to the floor.

Frank comes over and holds out a Freezie. Probably from his mini-fridge. "No stairs."

I take the stick of flavoured ice water. Grape. Mindy rolls herself in behind on a chair, the casters rattling on the raised floor. She has cherry. Seeing her suck on it throws my thoughts on a tangent for a few seconds before returning.

There must be something in the air, for Frank turns and stares at Mindy as well. She just sits on the chair, knees together and feet apart, sucking on the Freezie and staring at the ground. That is, until she looks up.

"What?" Mindy smiles with innocence, pushing the last of the cherry ice water up the plastic sleeve. "So, can we get down?"

The fuzz leaves me and I stand once again. "We're three stories up and the whole emergency staircase is in a jumble on the ground. Don't know what caused it, but there's a bunch of bodies mixed in with the metal."

Frank breaks out of his stupor. "I bet a bunch of them were climbing the thing, overloaded it, and down it came." He wacks a hand against a thigh.

"Gross." Mindy uses her feet to scoot the chair toward the door. "I wanna see."

She slides the chair up to the door and waits. I take the hint and push against the handle. The alarm sounds.

"Sorry," Frank says. He runs a few feet to a server rack, reaches up, and taps something. The alarm stops. "I bypassed the alarm in case I was late."

DOUGLAS OWEN

A visual of Frank rushing up the fire escape in order to sneak past our supervisor runs through my mind. I think the tilt sign on my forehead is a little too obvious.

"It's only three stories, Steve. I know you like driving and using the elevator but some of us try to actually exercise."

My throat tightens as I stifle a laugh. Mindy and Frank just stare at me. Once I settle, he flips me the finger, then walks down the row of servers. The crash of glass makes him stop. One glass brick was all it sounded like. A dull thump against the raised floor. But that's all it takes. I shake my head and step beside Frank, take his arm and lead him back to the door.

My voice shakes. "We need something to tie together or we'll never get out of here."

It's like I speak a different language. Frank starts to mumble to himself and Mindy scratches her head. Together we probably have an IQ just north of 400, and the common sense of a dung beetle. At least they have their shit together.

So we split up. Each going to different parts of the server room. Mindy lets out a squeak after a few minutes and runs to Frank. Guess he's the one she saw first. I glance to that area and a number of arms reach through the hole where the brick used to be. Several of the bricks around the opening shift a little as I watch. We need to get out of here. Now.

I find Frank and Mindy looking through the same boxes we each searched through before. They have extension cords and power bars strung together and plugged into each other. It takes a second but I realized what they're doing. Making a ladder with the power bars. The only problem – Frank weighs over 100 kg. Mindy could make it to the ground easily, maybe even me. Frank needs to lose weight if he has any hope in hell of using it.

But they keep working. Plug, wrap, pull, tug, and repeat. The whole thing looks laughable. But the jocks will never see it and neither will anyone else.

The jumbled mess soon stretches the length of the room twice over. I watch as Frank lifts one part and Mindy the other. They carry the makeshift ladder to the door and use more power bars to secure it to a rack. A few tugs later and Frank gives Mindy a high five. I just shake my head. Nerds.

The ladder holds. I go down, hand under hand. Not with grace, but at least I make it down. Fingers and hands reach out toward me, missing my leg by centimetres. I want to swat at them but vacant eyes show no emotion.

Mindy starts her decent, one step at a time. For someone as sure of herself while going under the floor, her movement down the ladder is painstakingly slow. I watch, not out of necessity but reflex when a pretty girl cannot tell you're watching.

She hits the ground and smiles.

"Come on, Frank!" she calls up.

I cringe and whisper, "Mindy, they're attracted by sound."

She slaps a hand over her mouth and words come out muffled. "Oh shit!"

Frank starts his downward climb and both Mindy and I hold our breath. I imagine the plugs coming out and Frank tumbling to the earth into the mix of shifting corpses and waiting mouths. Losing Frank would be a killer, and not something I want.

"Hurry," I whisper over and over again. And then his feet hit the ground.

We all stand on firm earth, smiling at each other. My car sits just a few metres away. I lead them. They follow. A body falls out of the door and lands with a splat where we were, parts of it impaled by twisted metal. A loud clanking sounds as another falls, but it stops moving. One long rebar sticks through its head.

"They're fucking lemmings." I pull keys from my pocket with a shaking hand.

Mindy points into the distance. "More are coming. Better hurry."

No gun. No nothing. Damn fire arm laws. We'd be better off if I had a gun, or at least my hunting bow. Then again, the number of people Frank usually pisses off during the day on his bike makes it better the laws are in place.

"Come on man," Frank mutters. "Get that door open and let's get out of here."

It's not like I don't want the door to open. The damn key is the problem. Usually use the remote. "Idiot!" I swear and press the open door button on the little transmitter. The only thing that works perfect on the damn car is the remote.

Mindy slips in the front and Frank pushes his bulk into the back. I press the clutch, jam the keys into the ignition, turn, and pray. A sputter.

"Come on," I whisper. The day is still hot and the windows all closed. We cook in the heat. Frank's deodorant must have given out on the climb, the smell of humanity reeks in the car. One more turn.

The car starts, stutters, almost stalls, revs up, smooths out. I let out a sigh.

"Get this shit-box rolling, Steve," Mindy says, her head toward the window.

Just a few steps away comes one of the student chefs, cleaver in one hand, bloody stump on the other side. His lumbering gait tells me what he is. The cleaver raises into the air.

"GO!" Frank screams.

The cleaver comes down. It hits the car just before the front window. I slam the gear into reverse and pop the clutch. The Focus screams, wheels spin, and we back up. Slow at first, then the tires grab. I shove it into first and take off down the parking lot, dodging the animated corpses as we go.

Mindy points out the front. At first I think it's just at the cleaver still embedded in the hood, but that's not right. As we approach the problem becomes clear. The gate bars our way out of the parking lot. And even though it is only wood, I drive a rusted-out Ford Focus. I remember the ground spikes they installed last year.

"Shit!" Yes, another intellectual masterpiece of a word.

I catch movement inside the guard house. A quick look behind shows a wall of animated death lumbering toward us. They didn't move fast, but it's a large wall of bodies able to just walk in a straight line, not dodging parked cars or following the road.

With not much time to decide on what to do, I step on the gas and pray.

The gate starts to lift, meaning the spikes must be down. Thank God! A womp and screech tell me the wooden arm scrapes against the roof on its way up. A head spins slowly in the guard house and some temp worker seems to wave. I swear to God he does.

We rise into the air and land back down on the road. Damn traffic calming hump at the end of the drive. My back bumper spins away in my rear-view mirror until it comes to rest by the curb. We skid a little before I get the car under control.

I think of all the routes to get home and decide the back roads would be better. Many cars jam the street, but at least they move. The sight of the highway, when we escaped Frank's room, told me to stay clear of them. I do.

Generally it takes me only 40 minutes to get home. Today, because of the traffic and lumbering bodies, I don't get there until the gas gauge light comes on. Seven litres left. Enough to get us one hundred kilometres if we only feather the thing in fifth gear.

My power still works. A quick hit of the remote and the garage door pulls up and out of the way. I back in. A quick swing of the wheel and roll forward. A yank on the parking brake locks the wheels. I pull out the key. The car sputters, knocks, and finally stops.

I put my head on the steering wheel.

Mindy stares straight forward.

Frank barfs.

My nose revolts. "Jesus! What the hell did you eat?"

As if to answer my question, he barfs again. Mindy and I open our doors and scramble out.

"I guess that means you'll be looking for a new car." She pulls at the bottom of her shirt, causing it to stretch over her small breasts.

Of course I look. Still alive doesn't mean not being a perv. She keeps the shirt stretched for a while and it dawns on me what she's doing. I look up and she's smiling.

"Sorry." I glance away after a good eyeful and knock on the rear passenger window. "You okay, Frank?"

If a black man could turn white, that is what Frank looks like. Eyes barely open, lips pale, and a small sheen of sweat on an otherwise shinny brow. "I'll be okay."

To show it, he barfs again. Thank God for the empty grocery bags in the back. It must be just about killing Frank in there. Maybe I can air the car out tonight or something. Right now, it's my only means of transportation in and out of the small town I live in.

I motion Mindy to the door with a hand. "I'll show you around."

She hesitates. "What about Frank?"

"He's been here before."

She nods and follows me into the house.

Air conditioning is wonderful. The blast of cold, about 22 °C, energizes me and puts a spring in my step. Samantha greets us at the door. Her feline howls for attention are nothing compared to the rasp of the tongue she uses on just about everything. The exaggerated black M on her forehead stands out against light brown fur.

The reaction Mindy has with the air becomes more entertaining than the pulling of her shirt. Another stare moment, but I look away before she sees me. At least I hope so. I feel heat on my cheeks.

Mindy bends down and picks up my little ball of fur. "Oh, she's so beautiful!"

"Samantha. Named after a witch." I smile. Chicks dig cats. They dig guys who like cats. Samantha got me laid a few years back before she porked out. Now, at just over 7 kg, her biggest accomplishment is jumping up on the bed at night.

"Can she wiggle her nose?"

For someone I think is just over twenty, Mindy is starting to impress me. "There's no way you can know that show."

She smiles. "My parents loved reruns. Helped teach them English."

I continue with the tour of my home, showing her everything from the kitchen to the upper floor TV room. For obvious reasons I steer clear of the bedrooms. Samantha trudges along behind us. We end up in the basement as the last stop. A mashing of wires run through the support joists with three massive Power Wall stations. I explain about going off the grid after the last big Liberal energy increase, cutting wood in the winter for the fireplace in order to help the geothermal furnace; powering everything from solar. Big investment, but worth every dime. I can run my air whenever I want without worrying about the cost. Even the winters are warm with the fireplace helping out. She nods, smiles, drools. It's a geek thing.

Mindy pulls out her cell and then looks at me. "What's the password?"

She wants the wi-fi password, something I rarely give out. Usually I have time to setup a guest access point to limit download speed and what they can see from my home servers. Today I didn't expect to bring anyone home with me.

Mindy sees my hesitation. "Sorry, just... well, my VOIP doesn't take up much bandwidth and I'd really love to check my mail with the network down."

It's against my better nature to disclose passwords. Working in IT, my guts twist when someone says they're going to write their password down. Come on, write it down? How about just giving someone the pin to your bank card? But then again, I've heard of people putting those on the signature strip.

I've never seen a cute girl beg. That's what she just about does. Hell, she seems about ready to let a tear run down a cheek. I give in. Tell her the password. I can always change it tomorrow. How many of these "corpses" can use their cell's anyway?

"Okay, but it's not connecting." Mindy holds out her phone for me to see.

"Oh, the 'bash' is not the word. I'm an old linux guy, it's the exclamation mark." Common mistake, that's why I always say it the way I do.

"It's connecting. Got signal. That's pretty strong. What are you using to keep the signal strength so high?" Her fingers dash over the cell's small screen.

"The power lines in the home do all the transmissions." I indicate the walls. "The whole house is a transmitter."

She nods. I think I just went up a few notches in her book.

"You think Frank's okay?"

I fall a few of those notches. "Should be." I scratch my head a little. "Let's get him cleaned up. It's the least we can do."

"Probably needs a change of clothes." Mindy follows me up the stairs.

"I don't think there's anything here for him to wear. I could have a look. Maybe he left something last time he had to sleep over."

"Why would he need to sleep here?"

"D & D party. Adults don't drink fruit juice."

She seems to get that, letting out a little giggle.

We make our way into the garage. Frank seems to be still barfing his guts out but that doesn't stop the little fire cracker from opening the door. The poor guy looks half dead.

Frank glances up at Mindy, tries to smile, fails, lulls his head and groans.

DOUGLAS OWEN

I saw Samantha corner a chipmunk one day. The little thing shivered and sputtered, trying to get away from the claws. When a gash was too much, and the blood almost out of its body, the thing seemed to give up on life and look at my cat with resignation to its fate. It was better than the look Frank holds in his eyes. At least the chick monk knew what was happening to it. I don't think Frank has a clue. None of us do. Mindy reaches into the car first. Not sure what she's thinking, all 40 kg of her. Frank tips the scale. It would take four Mindy's to even out the teeter totter, and even then I don't think it would level out. But she grabs his arm and gives a tug.

Frank helps. He raises a hand and pulls against the car door frame, his body straightening up just a little bit at a time. Then, he stands. Or should I say wavers.

I rush over before the guy topples to his knees.

"We need to get him inside." I can hardly believe the heat coming off Frank's body. "Crap, I think we need to get him to a hospital."

"No hospitals," Frank utters, his voice just barely above a whisper. "Just get me someplace to lie down."

"I don't know, Frank," Mindy says. She rushes ahead and opens the door. "If Steve thinks a hospital would be better then maybe we should get you to one."

"Don't think they'd be safe." His breathing settles down, as if he draws more strength by being pushed into movement. "The whole country's going to rat shit so the hospitals will be overrun with people."

Can't argue with his logic. The world does seem to be going to hell and we're just here for the ride. Maybe a lay down is all he needs. Mindy glances over and I look up, shaking my head.

Once inside the house and surrounded by cool air, he visibly relaxes. The bandage on his arm seems soaked with blood so I steer him toward the kitchen table. After a quick explanation of where to look, Mindy goes to the bathroom for bandages. She comes back and removes the blood soaked ones first.

I've seen a lot of crap. Heck, anyone with the internet has seen stuff from rough porn to tortured animals. I've never seen anything like the sight I see as the bandage comes off. Well, it doesn't really come off. Mindy pulls it off. Gently at first, then with a little more effort. Frank doesn't even wince. The skin looks ill, but nothing prepares me for the smell.

THE HORDES

Chicken in the Sun

Mindy covers her mouth. I take the bandage away from her and walk into the garage, holding back my stomach with every step. The bio-waste bucket sits on the ground just beside my old beat up truck that hasn't started since last year. I haven't tried to start the vehicle this year, didn't want the disappointment of the thing not running again. The bio container has a good seal, and we won't smell the rotten chicken again.

I toss the bandage and go back into the house to find Mindy trying to clean the wound. She has a roll of paper towel in one hand and a few gauze squares in the other. The latter she presses close to Frank's wound and pushes a little. A sickly yellow-green puss seeps out of the bite mark and she scoops it up. The smell intensifies when she does the action. Chicken left in the sun is all I can think of. That's not saying Frank smells like roses, no matter what his personal hygiene is like. We all spent too much time in my stinky little car.

"You have enough light?" I indicate the curtains drawn tight against the heat.

"Enough," Mindy says. She keeps pushing against the wound and more puss seeps out.

"Do you want any water?"

"Cold. Put ice in it if you can."

I really hate feeling useless. Sitting in front of a computer gives you the feeling of God, knowing at any time you could just press a button and send someone's personal information to anyone. Heck, there were a lot of things I could do at work. World of Warcraft beware! Frank and I control a number of groups. Crap, I had forgotten about the raid we setup for today. I glanced at the time. An hour past the meeting.

Ice clinks in the glass and water spurts out the fridge spout. I move on autopilot while thinking about the day. The glass almost reaches my lips before I remember it's for Mindy.

"Here." I hold out the glass.

"How's your arm feel, Frank?" Mindy presses the bandage against the bite waiting for Frank to respond.

"Better. Less pain." Frank takes a deep breath, flexes the fingers of his bit arm. "My fingers are a little numb."

"Could be nerve damage." I swear at myself for that one. Mindy glares at me from under her brow, an interesting trick for an Asian woman.

"Probably just the swelling," she says. "We should get some water into you."

"Rather have a pop." Frank wipes his brow. "Never really liked drinking water."

Mindy scowls. "Well, you'll drink it today."

I take the hint and get another glass.

"Thanks," Frank says, taking the water from me. "I'll try not to spill any."

Samantha jumps up on an empty kitchen chair, sits down, and stares at Frank. Her ears fold back and those lovely green eyes all but close. She lets out a hiss.

"Sam!" I glare at my cat. She jumps down and runs out of the kitchen, then thumps up the stairs.

Frank shook his head. "What's wrong with Samantha?"

"Who knows?" I walk back to the fridge and pour another drink, this time for me.

The way Samantha acted concerns me. Last time Frank came up to the house she fawned all over him. She even jumped up on his lap while we watched the game, something she never does with anyone. Something's wrong, and I'm punked if I know what it is.

Mindy says something but I don't catch it.

"Sorry?"

"I said do you have any more bandages?"

The thought whips through my mind. Probably, but where? "What

21

type?"

"Big ones." Mindy wipes more ooze off Frank's arm. "Think I got it cleaned out real good. Maybe some alcohol or something."

"Peroxide?" I'm sure some of that sits in a cupboard somewhere in the house.

"That'd do." Mindy presses another paper towel against Frank's arm and reaches for her glass. "And some more water."

It only takes a few minutes to find the peroxide, use it for cleaning printer heads. The bandages are another issue. I look all over to find something more than a simple kid's bandage, but nothing stands out. Not the stores in the kitchen or the bathrooms. Downstairs is a bust as well. Not one blood-stopping thing.

They're in the upstairs linen closet, up against the side the door folds into. Almost missed them if it wasn't for the big red cross on the package.

"Found some for you."

I wait a second, then decide just saying something was all I need to do. So down the stairs I go, seeing a four-legged ball of fur run into the closet I had opened. Fine, if she wants to be alone, let her.

Down the stairs and into the kitchen, I glance at the pile of grey-green paper towels on the table. Great, going to have to clean the table as well, not like the cat hasn't been sitting on it all morning, it gets the sun.

"Three sizes in this one." I put the box on the table and grab her glass. "Water or something stronger?"

I watch the internal struggle she goes through. Seems all kids love booze no matter who they are. "Got a beer?"

"I'll take a beer," Frank says.

"No!" Mindy and I say it at the same time. Frank winces.

To the fridge I go and pull out two beers from a micro-brewery I like. Something about the lime taste that gets me. Almost like an English pub beer. I crack the can and hand one over to Mindy. She takes it and smiles. The strange picture on the side makes her brow furrow but she doesn't say anything.

Frank drinks from his glass.

The bandage goes on fast. Mindy wraps it around his arm and ties it off with ease. The discolouring takes a little time to come through so I decide plastic sheets for Frank tonight.

Mindy checks her phone and frowns. "No signal."

I look over. "You on one of those small carriers in Toronto?"

"No, Bell." She swipes at her phone.

"Should be good. Did you connect to my network?"

She swipes the phone again. "Yeah, but the VOIP isn't working."

I dig out my phone, no connection except for the network. A few taps and I realize the outside is cut off. "No internet."

Frank has his phone out, an old dinosaur of a device. He flips it open and shows he has bars. "Old tech keeps working."

Mindy glances at him. "Can I use it to make a call?"

"Sure," Frank says, handing it to her. "Dial 9 to get an outside line." He laughs, then wheezes. "I gotta lay down, Steve. Where you want me?"

"Fold out in the front room." I point. "Let me get sheets on it first."

"I'll help," Mindy volunteers.

"Thanks."

We dig out the plastic sheets and setup the bed. Mindy puzzles over the choice but I mention Frank's wound discolouring the bandage and she nods. After a few minutes the bed holds the big guy and he's snoring softly. I motion for Mindy to follow me upstairs and into the TV room over the garage.

"Nice," Mindy says, looking at the TV again.

"Thanks." I pull out the modem and stare at the lights. The ones leading to the outside world all flash red, the others, green. No internet.

"High def?" Mindy stands before a couch now, eyeing the strange remote on the table.

"4K. Pick it up." I motion to the remote. "It's old, but easy to use."

With the power wall charged and the solar panels collecting, I wasn't too worried about the pull, even with the stereo. Mindy flips everything on and the room comes to life. I cover my ears from the blast of static coming through the speakers. Mindy winces as well.

"What is that?" Mindy tries to cover her ears and looks at the remote. She fails.

"You're on the sat, stopped on a wild feed I picked up last night." I stand and go over, expecting blood to be dripping from her ears. Nothing. "We have to change to over the air." I hit the remote. Sound dissipates. "Better. Flip through and see what's on. Try the news."

Mindy scans the stored channels, frowning at the lack of signal. All the major channels show us is black screen until we switch to the ancient ones. They show old fashion snow. The sound of hissing. Then she hits something. The picture still looks like we stare through a blizzard, but at least we can see it.

A man stands before us on the TV, his words mesh out every few seconds with the static. He proclaims, trumpets, and prostrates himself as the camera follows him along. An evangelist preacher. For some reason, all the channels, except this one, are off. I recognize this guy. His persona is always on the news about how he rips off seniors and seduces the interns. Not a nice character.

We both stare at the screen, hypnotized by the dancing static, hearing only half of what he says. Apocalypse. Hellfire. The dead. Evil. The dialogue goes on as he either thumps a fist into his hand or on the bible. I shake my weary head.

A quick motion to the control breaks Mindy out of the hypnotic preacher. "Nothing else on?"

Mindy scans the channels again and the only one we pick up is the reverend. I hold out a hand and Mindy puts the remote in it. A few minutes later, the TV has scanned the airwaves finding only that channel.

"I'll switch to the sat." The system flips to the small dish on the roof and I scan. Hundreds of scrambled channels show up.

"A lot to choose from," Mindy says.

I change the view and only twelve channels show. "These are the unscrambled ones on Nimiq 1."

Lots to see there. Some fireplace channel, the Canadian Parliament channel, a few other free for now channels and the news.

Crap! The news? I almost missed it.

The station came in off the satellite in dazzling clarity. I turn up the volume once the feed clears. The low tone buzz makes my back teeth vibrate as the words "This is the Emergency Broadcast Signal. Please stand by," flashes on the screen. We wait. And wait.

"I don't think anything is going to happen," Mindy says.

The back of her hand brushes against mine. Amazing what life and death can do to people in such a short time. I glance at her, but she keeps those beautiful eyes staring at the screen.

"I'm sure something will—"

The screen goes black for a second. A rustling of papers comes through the speakers and soon the picture splashes on in full HD quality. I gape at the background images of bodies sprawled on the ground, people shooting into crowds, and the general loss of humanity.

It must've been a live transmission; no one goes in front of a camera to read the news looking as disheveled as this man, but there he sits. The slight shadow across his chin tells us of how long the day has been. I can see the light trace of circles under eyes, far too young to have such. Hands shake as they pick up a few pieces of paper, then put them down. As a thought, he reaches for the glass of water, but the tremors continue to cause his hands to spill it on the papers he had just put down. He clears a dry throat and begins to speak.

"I'm Peter Michaels of the National News Service, sitting in for Philip Jahad. Today, we are a nation under siege." His breath slows as the few years of training he had kicks in and takes over. "The world is under siege. The Centre for Disease Control in the United States has announced an outbreak affecting North America and Mexico. We're still waiting confirmation from the Public Health Agency of Canada.

"The CDC is warning people to be wary of those stricken by this disease. They may be your loved ones, but being infected takes their mental competence away from them. They may attack you. Be careful of their bite or bodily fluids. If infected, please advise your family and law enforcement. Please do not attempt to enter a hospital, they are currently on lock down in order to protect those who are the weakest among us."

Mindy recovers first. "Jesus!" She squeezes my hand hard. "I really need to talk to my mom." Frank's phone is in her hand again and a small thumb dances across the numbers. It goes to her ear, then down again. She hits the numbers one more time and repeats.

I watch her brow furrow and the corners of her mouth sink. It takes a while for me to see the tear.

"Hold on, what's wrong?" I put a hand on her shoulder.

"Lines are down." She sniffles.

"That's nothing new." I'm really good at helping people feel better. "If the main cell lines are down then the hard lines are probably as well."

Her eyes lift a little and the sparkle is almost back. "You think so?"

I can feel the paint drying around me as I sit in the corner with a dripping brush. "Suuuuurrrre." Samantha rubs against my leg. I bend down and pick her up, offering the little bundle of fur to her. "Cat?"

The giggle tells me I hit the right nerve. She takes Sam out of my hands and hugs the little motor boat. "I never had a pet when I was a kid."

"Hell, you can have her. Keeps me from cleaning the litter box."

The announcer clears his throat and I look over. He's a little less worse for wear but still not that presentable. The set behind him shows several people moving about and a nearby security guard.

"Things are happening that you need to know." He glances to the left. "I know how this will sound, but it has to go out there. The dead are coming back to life."

Another person comes on screen, but his back is turned to the camera. "Pete, you need to stop. They'll pull us."

"Jesus!" I stare at the screen.

"Must be bad if the government is censoring it," Mindy says.

"Jeff, it doesn't matter anymore. The people need to know what is going on." He turns back to the camera. "People, listen to me. The dea–" The signal freezes, blotches. I swear. "–don't try to a he–" Again, we lose signal.

Mindy glances at me. "What is he trying to say?"

"–when you come across someone bitten, ju–"

I flip the channel up and down. The station is still there, but something is trying to block it. "Seems like their signal is being interrupted by something." A few steps to the right and I look out the window. Clouds are rolling in from the west. Dark, nasty weather clouds. "Looks like a storm's coming in."

"–nd try to keep safe. Lock yourselves in a secure home. Don't let anyone in who shows sig–" Pixelisation covers the screen. "–the brain– it stops the–base of the ne–though the ey–don't bu–spinal co–just bod– head trama–" The picture finally gives out to a black screen.

The summer storm rolls in. Wind picks up and light fades. "This is going to be a good one." I turn off the TV. "Best to wait it out. I have movies and such we can watch."

Mindy stares at the TV. "Maybe we should look in on Frank. Make sure he's okay."

"Good idea." I start to head for the stairs. "You coming?"

"In a sec."

"You okay?" There's a welling of moisture in her eyes. Crap, I hate it when chicks cry. "If you want to lay down..."

She wipes at her eyes, gives a little smile, and fights back the invisible demons. "I'll be all right. Just thinking."

I nod. She walks toward me. Down the stairs we go and into the living room.

Fred is sprawled on the fold out. He's still sleeping, even with the sound of the rain. Summer storms can get pretty brutal here. The small town I live in is kind of in a cauldron of sorts. Way back in the early 1800's it used to flood, that is before they put in drainage ditches and paved roads. Now I just get a little water in the basement when a storm is out of the east.

Mindy walks up beside the bed and puts a hand on Frank's forehead. Gingerly, she then pulls back the green stained bandage on his arm. She shakes her head and glances at me.

"I cleaned that well, but it seems to be just as swollen as before."

I come up beside her and look down. The chicken-left-in-the-sun smell slams into me so hard I almost gasp. "His arm looks bad."

Mindy touches around the wound. "Yeah. We should really get him some medical help." She puts the bandage back in place. "I'm not a doctor, but I know an infection when I see one."

Images of my friend losing his arm floats unbidden to my consciousness. Frank would not like that if it happened. Heck, I wouldn't like him to go through that, but what can you do if they decide it needs to be removed in order to save your life?

"Is there anything we can do?" Ask questions. Hunt for an answer. Just like programming. Follow a plan to fix the issue.

She takes a deep breath. "Nothing that I can do. Basic first aid. Mom and Dad wanted me to be a doctor, but dealing with sick people gives me the creeps."

Something I can relate to. I look out the window. "Don't think we're going anywhere soon." Lightning lights up the sky. A few seconds later, thunder rolls across the landscape. I look at Frank. His snore answers me. "Looks like he's at least getting some sleep. You hungry?"

"Rather have another beer."

"That can be arranged."

Bump in the Night

We sit and talk in the TV room. Mindy says a lot about her family and how they wanted her to be a doctor. At the fifth beer, my cheeks are tingling and the world starts to make sense. Funny how everything is better with a few beers in you.

The storm keeps pouring down. When the room becomes really dark, I turn on a light and look outside, announcing it to be night time and head to bed. I tell Mindy about the spare bedroom and where to find extra sheets. At least I think I tell her that.

The rain stops sometime during the night and a strange thumping sound wakes me up. It's just my head from all the beers. I stumble to a standing position, still groggy, but nothing a good brushing of the teeth won't fix.

Mindy is curled up with me. Her olive shin glints in the pre-dawn light and I wonder how far we went. It's hard to tell, I like commando. It appears she does as well.

I try to extract myself from our intertwined bodies, feeling myself stir as hands touch the soft skin of her breasts. The biggest problem is my right arm, and Mindy's head resting on it.

A pillow in one hand and the other balancing Mindy's head, I pull away slow, making sure not to jostle her in any way. Long, silky hair follows but the pillow slides under her head and I let out a silent cheer of achievement before slipping my feet out and onto the floor.

Curiosity gets the best of me and I lift the sheet just a little to look at her naked back, then down to her butt. I give myself a mental high five and let the blanket fall back down against her body.

My comfy pants are by the bed so I slip them on, and push reluctant feet into slippers. The clock beside the bed reads 4:45 a.m., just a few minutes before sunrise. Time to put on some coffee.

Mindy's voice breaks the silence and I stop. "Black, three sugars."

"You're supposed to be asleep."

She giggles a little, not rising, but I see the outline of an arm coming up to her head. "What? And miss the show?"

I blush, it's one thing to look, but getting caught is another. "Three sugars?"

"Yes. And something for my head, it's pounding."

There's a thudding noise downstairs, as if someone hit the dining room table. Samantha runs into the room and jumps up on the bed, ears flat, a low growl comes out as she looks toward the door. Her hair is puffed out.

Mindy sits up, sheet falling from her body. "What's wrong with Samantha?"

I look to her, look at the cat, look at her. The light is growing and I can see her even better now. I try looking into Mindy's eyes, but my gaze falls a little south. She giggles. Another thump. Her smile disappears. Samantha growls again.

"Must be Frank. Probably thinks he's an elf and can see in the dark. I'll make some coffee." Hesitation as she looks at my lower body. I glance down to see my soldier standing at attention. Again, heat rises to my cheeks. "Better get out of here to settle him down."

She giggles again, grabs Samantha, and dives back under the covers.

I turn and head to the stairs, making my footfalls loud so Frank knows I'm coming. With a force of will, I think about my boss naked and my arousal dies, quick, but my stomach almost hurls at the image. Going to have to remember that trick in the future.

"Frank?" There's only silence, then a groan. "I'm coming down to make some coffee, want any?"

Two steps down.

"You okay, Frank?"

Four steps down.

"Frank, answer me, will you?"

Six steps and I peer at the fold out. Sheets are crumpled into a mass around a dark form. He's still laying there, but his leg is draped over the edge of the bed to the floor. It thuds against the floor making the sound we heard upstairs.

I'm a coward. Scared of the dark. Dash upstairs when I turn off the lights so the boogie man doesn't get me. Stuff like that. I rush toward my friend and stop a few paces away. The sheets are smeared with the green gunk that came from his arm yesterday. I pull back a sheet and see the puss also covers his body. An arm, once recognizable, is bloated, puffy, and a bluish tint runs its length. Instead of part of his arm looking ghastly, the whole thing gives off a harrowing growl of anger to my senses.

"Frank."

His breath is ragged and gurgles as if he is drinking from a straw with only drops at the bottom of the glass.

Frank shakes, starts to convulse. I reach out with fumbling hands and attempt to stop him from hurting himself. Crap, he's burning up. The heat coming off him is tremendous. The sun would have a hard time warming him this high. The gurgling in his chest grows. He shits himself. The smell is sickening and hits me like a train. I swallow back bile. And as fast as the convulsions start, they stop. His breath rattles out. There is no more struggling or movement. Nothing.

"Frank!"

I shake his shoulders. His head lops to the side. Spittle mixed with blood foams in his mouth and I know we've lost him. I sit on the edge of the bed and hang my heavy head. We were friends. Maybe not the best of friends, but still friends. World of Warcraft and Pokemon and just about any kind of game you could imagine. He even tried to teach me dominoes once.

Mindy comes down the stairs and stops. "I heard yelling..." She's carrying Samantha who struggles to get free. One of my old flannel shirts covers her from shoulders to knees, but the front is only buttoned a little. She sits on the stairs and Samantha jumps free of her grasp. I could only imagine the tableau we form.

It lasts a while. Me sitting on the edge of the bed, Mindy on the stairs, Samantha hiding somewhere, Frank decomposing slowly beside me. I remember some of the pranks he used to pull at work. Little things like changing a small line in someone's email signature or making a rom drive open on them. Little things like that to make a person smile.

The brief reflection ends and I stand. A quick tug and the blanket covers Frank's body. I bend my head and mutter a silent prayer for my friend before going to the kitchen. The cat food is in a jar and I scoop out some for Samantha, wondering where she is. This is her happy time. Food time. But my cat seems to have abandoned us. I still fill her bowl and put it down.

Small arms encircle my waist and the press of a body bears on me. I'm not sure what to do, but something has to happen. I reach down and touch one hand. Her body shakes against mine and sniffling sounds fill the room. Maybe something else is wrong but for now all I can think of is getting coffee ready.

"I don't think I could eat." She rubs her head against my back.

A realization comes over me. This woman is bonding to me. I've had girlfriends before, but nothing like this one. She is pretty, smart, sexy, hot. I think we had sex and I never really bought her dinner or took her to a show. How the hell did that happen? The world is a strange place.

I reach for the coffee urn and grinds. Spill in two scoops. Put it down. Pick up the kettle and fill it with water. Plug it in. Wait.

Her arms tighten around me.

"We have to eat." Thoughts of what to make go through my mind. "Then take him outside."

The squeezing stops.

I take a deep breath. "It's not something I want to do either, but we can't leave him in here much longer. The heat…"

Her voice almost breaks. "When?"

"Soon. After breakfast."

"Okay, but nothing big." She squeezes me again.

I push away from the table. Mindy has an appetite and already packed away six pancakes and half a pack of bacon. She eats like someone starving, shovelling forkful after forkful into her mouth. Her coffee is black with three sugars. Sweet, but not overpowering, just like her. How the hell does she stay so skinny?

We talked during breakfast. She's a second generation or CBC as she calls it, Canadian born Chinese. Parents live in Toronto, downtown, where they run a sushi restaurant. She works there in the summer and goes to school the other times. Like she said, they wanted her to be a doctor but it was not in her future. She loves drama and the arts. The biggest claim to fame, she admitted, a commercial spot that aired last winter.

"Got milk?" She laughs and just keeps scooping more food into her mouth.

I stand, motion to the dwindling supply of pancakes. "Do you want more?"

Her fork dashes out faster than the eye can see and the last two are on her plate. A quick movement and maple syrup is poured over them.

"This is enough." She forks another pancake into her mouth, chews, and swallows. "What?"

"I've just never seen anyone eat so much." I take the empty plate from the centre of the table. "Frank says—"

She stops eating. I can't believe I just said that. Frank is still on the pull out, covered by the blanket. Mindy's lower lip starts to tremble.

"I'm sorry." The plate shakes as my hand quivers. "It's just hard to believe he's gone."

Mindy nods, then looks down at the last two pancakes cowering on her plate. "Some cultures bury food with the recently deceased so they have something to eat."

I nod this time. "Sounds like a plan." My scheme for the backyard was almost complete. Just a few more places left to smooth out. But why in the first part of the back? Heck, my property is almost an acre so we could bury Frank just about anywhere. I have plastic to wrap around his body. Keep the animals from eating any part of him.

Images of my friend being dug up by coyotes run through my mind. Their teeth ripping and tearing at his flesh. It makes me sick to think his grave could be desecrated so easily just because I live in a rural area. No, we'll bury him, wrapped in plastic.

"Have you tried your phone yet?" I pull my own out and check for signal. Nothing.

"This morning. No signal." She sits back, lets out a deep breath. "I wish I knew what was going on with my parents."

"I'm sure something will be up later today." I go to the sink, put the dishes in it, and stare at Samantha's bowl. "Things are just a little weird right now."

"No shit." Mindy gets up and puts her plate on the counter.

I reach down, open a cupboard, and pull out a sandwich bag. The pancakes go into it.

It takes us the better part of an hour to haul Frank's body out of the house. Most of that is my fault.

We tried carrying him by arms and legs, just like the old-style grave diggers did. But a dead body is limp, offering no resistance. He slips from our arms and hits the floor. We try again and the same result. No one told me a limp body is hard to carry.

I put the sheet on the floor and together we roll him onto it. Then we drag him through the kitchen and out into the yard. Ten minutes of pulling and we have him exactly where I measured out. I remember something he said to me last year about two feet in either direction and five feet from another, so I pick one of the birch trees and paced out five steps before digging.

They used a backhoe in order to level out part of my back yard. Rocks litter the ground not too far down, so they're a pain. I keep hitting them with each shovel full of dirt. At least I can somewhat muscle them out. Mindy is helping with another shovel and stops just about all the time to see if she got a rock. Thankfully, they are usually small enough to pry out of the ground.

Mindy straightens up, pushes hair from her eyes and looks around. "There's no road noise."

"Sorry?"

"Cars. I don't hear any cars."

I stop digging. Nothing. No dump trucks heading to the pits just north of me. Wind, yes; but vehicles, no. Even in this rural neighbourhood there should be cars running back and forth, I'm just a stone's throw from one of the highways, small though it is.

"Yes, silence." I relish in the moment, then realization slaps my across the face and brings me back to reality. "Silence. Not even a plane or car." Very disturbing. I rub the back of my neck, let the shovel drop, step out of the hole we started. "People should be moving about."

"Come to think of it, I didn't even see any lights on anywhere last night." Mindy drops her shovel and steps out of the hole as well. "What could it mean, Steve?"

"Not sure." I mull it over in my head. Even the bakery on the corner has a backup generator. It should have fired up by now. "I think I'm going to knock on a few doors."

We finish digging the grave for Frank. I can hardly move. Never been one for a lot of exercise. Now I can hardly lift my arms. It takes all my energy to climb into bed.

Mindy slips in beside me, cuddles up, and my mind goes wild. Do I have a girlfriend? A hot girlfriend? An Asian, hot, girlfriend? The guys on the forums will go wild with this news.

I squeeze Mindy closer and she responds. One leg comes around and she's all of a sudden on top of me. Her hair falls and covers us as we kiss.

We make love. Softly at first, then heat, desire, passion, and the desire to forget the death of someone builds the fury.

I spend inside her and she collapses, all forty kilos of her. Then the tears start again. I keep holding her, stroking her back, hair, giving cooing sound. It works after a while and Mindy slips off me, her back toward me.

A small thought clicks in my head; does she want me to snuggle up or not? You see it on the movies all the time. Man and woman have sex. Woman snuggles to man. If the woman doesn't snuggle to the man, she wants to be left alone. But then again, she may just want me to reach around and hold her. How could I know what she wants me to do? Life, so unfair for the uninitiated.

I struggle. Will she shrug me off? Feel comforted? Reject the intimacy? After what we just did… Decisions. I mentally flip a coin. Flip another. Then realize I've already made up my mind. I roll over and snuggle against her. One arm drapes over and, trying not to hit her breast, rests on her shoulder. Mindy responds by inching against my body. Right move. I feel like a stud, a rock star. Conquer of Worlds.

Her hair still has the wonderful scent of wild flowers about it. Not overpowering, but just enough to notice. Her breathing steadies. I allow myself a mental picture before falling asleep.

Samantha's hiss wakes me. I'm still tangled up with one arm around Mindy, whose steady breathing tells me she still sleeps, but nothing gets a cat owner going more than the sound of their animal growling and hissing. Even with the night slowly retreating before the morning sun, I can just see her eyes wide, tail puffy, ears flat against her head.

I hear a thud.

The sound makes my bladder scream to be emptied.

Another thud echoes. This one louder, then the sound of a gate being pushed open. Then another thud sounds, followed closely by another. The sound is as if someone is bouncing off the patio door.

I whip off the blankets. Samantha jumps, runs to the head of the bed. She must have hit something tender for Mindy moans and rolls over.

"What's... noise?" She yawns. "What's that noise?"

"Don't know." I pull on pants. "Get dressed, just in case."

Mindy rolls out of bed, throws on some pants as well as one of my shirts, and scoops Samantha up. The cat decides being carried is not in the plans for today. She squirms, backs up, escapes under Mindy's arm. Clawed feet scramble across the bed, hit the floor, and retreat down the hall.

"Damn, I think she got me," Mindy says.

The room is brighter, or I've adjusted to the low light. Either way, I glance over and see a long, red line across Mindy's forearm. No blood.

"Just a scratch." I turn my attention to the bedroom door and force one foot in front of the other.

The thudding gets louder.

A bright light blazes behind me.

"Fuck!" It's a whisper, but still, my voice breaks the monotony of the thudding.

The light goes off.

"What?"

"Okay, wait a sec, my eyes have to adjust." The solid white dot in my eyes start to fade and I swear Mindy is blushing. She puts the flashlight in a pocket and steps beside me.

"I'll be more careful next time." She takes my hand.

"Don't worry." I bend down to kiss her.

There is more than urgency in the kiss. More like a desire to be together. Only two days and the bond is similar to that of the one Samantha and I created when she first came home with me.

Another thud and I end the embrace. "I'll find out what that's all about, then we can figure out what to do today."

DOUGLAS OWEN

She sits on the bed. "Maybe fix up Frank's grave."

I head toward the door. "Yes, that's a good idea."

Mindy follows me out of the bedroom, through the hall, and down the stairs. A quick glance through my octagonal window shows the back gate open.

"We closed the gate yesterday, didn't we?"

Mindy grunts out a positive.

I step up out of the mud room and glance to the kitchen first. A gasp escapes Mindy.

"What's wrong…"

My mind stops working. There is something definitely wrong with the sight we see. I rub tired eyes and step forward. My hand taps the light switch. The backyard floods with illumination. Milky eyes stare through the patio door directly at me without seeing.

Mindy screams as I step back, away from the walking corpse of Frank.

A Friend in Death

I bump into the kitchen table, wondering what sick joke is taking place. Frank hits its head against the patio door again. Small smudges of dirt decorate the glass and the skin above his eyebrow breaks. No blood seeps out. He's oblivious of the injury. His once dark eyes are pale and blotchy as they move toward me. I want to heave, but cannot take my gaze off my friend.

Mindy sits on the floor, head in hands, weeping. It must be shock.

"He's alive. We buried him alive," she mutters.

"No, his body was cold." I can't keep my eyes off of the animated corpse before us. There's a definite icy claw on my spine. "What the hell did the newscaster say on that broadcast?"

She lifts a tear filled gaze at me. "What?"

"Monday, when all hell broke loose." I wonder if my hunting gear is upstairs or down, locked or just hanging.

Another thud pulls my attention back to the patio door.

"He'll break in!" Mindy slides back to the floor.

"No, it's tempered glass, just like all the windows." It cost a bundle when the upgrade happened last year, but the savings in heat is phenomenal. "They said something about the brain." Nothing isclicking in my mind.

Mindy sniffs. "You have to kill the brain." She wipes away tears with an arm. "Probably the brain stem or cerebellum."

I'm stunned. "How the hell—"

She shudders. "Remember, Mom and Dad wanted me to go to med school, so they drilled me on anatomy all the time." She climbs to her feet. "We have to let him in. Maybe there's something…"

I shake my head. "No. The announcer said something about the infection."

"We can't leave him out there."

"Not like that." I remember my hunting bow is in the basement. Dad always made sure I knew how to hunt, and he hated guns. Without waiting for her response, I make my way into the basement. The morning light still isn't enough to brighten up downstairs, so I flick on the light.

At the bottom of the stairs, I spy the compound bow. It takes a second to restring it, and another to grab three arrows with razor heads on them. With over sixty-five pounds of draw weight, it should do the trick.

I turn off the lights while climbing the stairs. Frank is still at the patio door. There's nothing in his eyes. Those usually inquisitive black orbs are covered with a white mist, telling me nothing's behind them anymore. But I still hesitate. What if the announcer was wrong? There may still be something of my friend there, hiding behind the lumbering body. I decide to go around the house.

The front door is locked, so it takes a second to flip the deadbolt and unhook the chain. Then a hand touches me. I jump. How did he—

Mindy has a hand against her chest. "Oh, my God. Sorry."

There's something that needs to be said, but it just doesn't want to come out. The geek in me has a desire to just run and hide behind a keyboard, use the anonymity of the internet to shield my thoughts, or just pretend and let a blank screen stare at me. But there's something in her eyes. It has to come out.

"I can't let him suffer like that." The hunter in me, the one Dad took so much time to train before his death, comes out in a torrent of self-confidence. But this is my friend. What if he's still Frank? The person who was always there to support me. Maybe my best friend.

No. Nothing of the man I once knew appears to be behind those milky eyes. "I need to protect those around me, including you."

A small smile forms in her eyes. It reaches to the corners of her mouth and she takes my free hand. Nothing needs to be said. There's a connection between us. Something that has formed over these two days.

Another thud against the patio door breaks the spell. I lean forward, kissing her softly. "I want to see if there's anything of Frank left in that shell before…"

"And if there's not?" Her voice is soft, wondering, with a little concern rounding the edges. The smile is gone now, and a tear threatens to escape her left eye.

"Then one of these will end it." I hold up an arrow. "And we'll bury him again. Hopefully for the last time."

She stares at the weapon in my hand. A thud and moan makes her jump. "Then you need to show me how to do it as well."

The back is open and I motion for Mindy to follow. We sneak to the gate and push it a little more.

Frank is still thudding against the patio door, pushing harder this time. There's clumsiness about his movements. A puppet with some of the strings cut. But something tells me there's nothing controlling him. No thought. No desire. No passion. An empty, animated, decaying husk once known as my friend.

I turn to Mindy, voice low. "Keep silent."

One foot forward. Then another. I pass the gate, one arrow nocked.

"Frank," I call out.

The shell that was once my friend stops banging against the door and turns with slow deliberation. There's no recognition. I pull back the bow.

This is not a deer. Not a moose. Not a bear. It's a person. My friend. Someone I've eaten and laughed with. Hell, I work with the man. But he's not a man.

This creature walking toward me is a corpse. I buried him just yesterday. He should not be walking. There's no breath, but he moans. His hand reaches out as he walks a few paces toward me.

"Frank, don't come any closer. Tell me what happened."

He just moans, taking another step forward. A mouth full of teeth opens wide. Dirt covers his clothes and pale skin is underneath that. There are cataracts in his eyes, giving them that milky look. The stare makes my bladder shrink.

There is a moment in every hunter's life when they hesitate. It happens on their first kill, and if they don't train it out, it returns for every kill after that. It can cause them to miss the shot. Or worse yet, it could cost them their life, depending on what they're hunting.

"Steve!"

I wake out of the trance with Mindy's shout. Frank is almost on me. His hand reaches out. I bring the bow up and pre-dawn light glints off the three-bladed head. I loose the arrow.

What was I thinking? One shot would take him down? Yes, that was what I thought. But putting an arrow into my friend, into Frank, is not something I thought of doing when I woke up. It's a final note. The point that tells me the world has gone to shit. And now I have to figure out how to survive.

My arrow leaves the bow. It flies true. Impacts Frank in the mouth, enters, and exits the back of his head and drops to the ground ten feet behind his lumbering body. Mindy lets out a squeak. I nock another arrow, pull back just as Frank's hand touches the bow. This one flies perfect. The point hits the middle of his forehead and lodges there. The moaning stops. Lifeless eyes stare unblinking at me. Then, without ceremony, his body crumples to the ground.

"Is he dead?" Mindy is shaking as she takes my arm.

"Yeah, I think so." Shit, I hope so. That's something I don't want to do again. Just to make sure, I poke at Frank with the end of my bow. Nothing. "He's dead."

"What now?"

I let out a sigh. "We bury him. Again."

It hits me then. I'm such an idiot. All that work lugging the body and what we needed was just over in the corner. I take Mindy's hand and walk us over to the south side of the yard where I keep the wheelbarrow.

Even dead, Frank still weighs a good 140 kg. Hard enough to lift, but we manage. The earth of his grave doesn't take long to move, but this time we dig a little deeper. Funny how you think of such things when circumstances warrant.

We dump his body, cover it, and make it back to the house. Mindy tries to call her parents again but the cell lines are still down, no signal. Even the internet is still down. We scan all the regular airwaves for something, but there's nothing except a pixelated test signal out of Buffalo. We stare at it for a few minutes, hoping it changes to a person, or something. It doesn't.

Not wanting to think humanity is gone, I turn on the satellite and program it to scan for wild feeds. It first swings the small Ku dish to EchoStar 18 and runs through the frequencies. I stare for a few minutes.

"What's it doing?"

I look over at Mindy; she's sitting on the edge of the couch just watching the numbers. Her brow is pulled together and those beautiful eyes are squinting.

"Wild feed scan." I sit beside her, and place an arm around those wonderful shoulders. "It'll step through all the possible frequencies one at a time, mark anything that is sending, then switch to the next sat and do the same thing."

"How many?"

"Around ninety. I was going to upgrade to the set that actually scans for new sats when they come in, but that..." The shop. Frank and I were going to go there next week, upgrade. The thought of Frank sitting in the ground now just about breaks me. A small hand touches my cheek and I let it guide me to look into deep, dark pools of brown.

"You did what you needed to do." Mindy uses her thumb to stroke my cheek. "He was coming at you. There's no telling what would have happened if you didn't put him down."

"Or if he would have done anything."

"He would have." She glances away for a second. "I've seen that kind of action from people in the past. Just blind animal instincts. They want something, and there's no way they're going to let it get away from them."

"But it was Frank! My friend." I want to say best friend, but something stops me from trying to humanize the walking corpse like that. "There could have been a way to bring him around—"

"No, don't you second guess yourself like that," Mindy snaps at me. "If you do that we're done." She stands, places both hands on her hips. "You hunt, right?"

"Yes, a little. My Dad—"

"And did he teach you to hesitate when killing your prey?"

"No, hesitation kills the shot, or the hunter depen—"

"So why do you want to humanize Frank? If he comes out of the ground this time, then what kind of shot will take him down? Will we need to cut off his head or something?"

I just stare at her.

"Something you may want to know, Steve, is that my parents, backward as they are, came to Canada and settled here before I was born. I know what they went through in order to escape China. That's something they told me about." She is staring at me, eyes blazing with the truth of her words. "They lived in a small town just outside of

Dartmouth where they ran a small restaurant."

I want to blurt out a Chinese food restaurant but those wonderfully dark eyes told me the possible anger she'd have for something like that. My teeth clamp down on my tongue.

"They raised chickens and goats at home, slaughtering them for our own food while feeding the crap chicken to the white people all around them. If they thought of those people as human, then they would not have made enough to move to Toronto, or send me to college, even though I didn't choose to go to med school."

Her gaze slides off me and to the floor. I start to open my mouth.

"I'm not finished." She takes a deep breath. "Now the world is gone to shit, and the one guy who I bump into is the nicest, smartest, most prepared person I have ever known." Her face softens, the hard squint in her eyes is gone, a smile even starts to lift one corner of her mouth. "And he seems to like me as well. Didn't even throw me out of bed the first night." Her smile is wide now. "And has a tender heart." She steps forward and kneels on the floor in front of me, taking both my hands. "And he is tender, caring, nice, and has the cutest little dimples when he smiles."

I swim in those eyes.

"And he seems to really like me."

Her soliloquy does me in. There's nothing I can do to stop myself. I lean forward and kiss her.

I flip a pancake, then move some of the bacon over to the other side of the griddle. Mindy watches as the little pieces of meat candy fry up, releasing a sweet aroma into the air. The table is set, so there's nothing left for her to do but wait until the morning meal is ready.

The sat scan finished a few hours ago and we did pick stuff up, but all the signals came in encrypted. Without the internet, I couldn't pull the keys to decrypt them. So I left it on scan, hoping something would come in over time.

We went to bed early after that and made love. Yes, made love, not screwed like horny kids. We seem to have tipped our relationship to something of that nature. I didn't just get my rocks off, though that did happen, and Mindy made sure she enjoyed it as well. But there was a tenderness about it. Slow. Deliberate. A true want to please the other person more than have our own desires met. I guess that's why they call it making love instead of fucking. One is just a selfish desire and the other is a want and need to put someone else first.

And after a wonderful night's sleep and no work to go to, I pulled out some bacon from the freezer and decided to treat us.

Mindy takes in a good sniff of the cooking food. "Everything smells wonderful." She's wearing another one of my shirts. It's white, and does nothing to hide her breasts when she sits up.

"My dad taught me how to make pancakes years ago."

I let my mind wander back to when I was seven. Dad mixing the batter and explaining how you need to cook bacon in order to have the perfect pancake. "You need bacon grease or you don't have pancakes." He always loved his bacon, and I do as well, just because it reminds me of him.

"Where were you?" Mindy waves a hand in front of my face.

"Sorry, just remembering my Dad." I flip another pancake, but it burned just a little on the underside. Damn. "He taught me how to make pancakes and I adjusted the receipt to my own liking."

"So, you mean to say everything you learned was from him?"

I chuckle a little. "No, not everything." Bacon is pushed around, letting the grease coat the griddle. "He taught me about cooking and hunting. Things like how to treat a woman. When to fart in public and when not to."

Mindy giggles. It seems everyone likes a good fart joke.

"When to hold a door open and when not to. How to memorize, speak to people, treat them with respect, and how not to judge someone because they're different."

"Sounds like a nice man." Mindy seems fixated on the bacon.

"Yes, he was."

"Was?" Mindy glances up, brow pulled together.

"Yes, passed away about five years ago." I take a deep breath. Talking about my father still leaves me feeling at a loss. "Cancer. Never smoked a day in his life but got lung cancer."

"Sorry to hear that." Mindy turns her head. "If you don't—"

"No, that's okay." I take another deep breath. "It was a while ago and maybe talking to you about it will help keep his memory alive."

I grab a little paper towel, look at the cardboard tube on the holder as three sheets come free. Need more. "He said it's better to be prepared than need something." I put the paper towel on a plate, place some bacon on it so the grease is absorbed. "I guess that's why he hunted. Get your own meal from Mother Nature's butcher shop."

I put pancakes on another plate, move three slices of bacon from the right side of the griddle to the left, and pour out more batter. "We kept a good larder at the house, and at the cottage. Could go for weeks without having to shop unless it was for eggs or something." I put the last of the bacon on the plate, notice two slices are already gone from the four I placed there earlier. "We'll need to make a run into the gas station."

"How far is it?"

"Oh, just down the tracks and two houses over. Not even a klick." I unplug the griddle and put the last of the pancakes on the plate. We both walk to the table and sit down. "We can walk, but maybe taking the car would be a good thing. If this un-dead thing is for real, we'll need to stock up on stuff." I take four pancakes and bacon slices, put them on my plate. Mindy scoops up the rest. Hell, she can eat.

"I'm not sure what they have in stock or if there's anyone there, but it doesn't hurt to find out." I think of the Indian couple who own the station. All that work, day in and day out.

"What if it's locked?" Mindy stuffs another pancake into her mouth.

"There's always ways to get into a place."

She nods.

"Besides, best to take advantage of having it near before someone else finds it."

Another nod. Her plate's half eaten. I look down and see one pancake and strip of bacon missing from the four. Something tells me I ate them while talking but don't remember doing it.

"So, we take your car?"

"Until we can get you one."

Her fork stops midway to mouth. "I don't think I could drive."

I've seen it before. People in accidents who stop driving, especially if someone's injured. I'm concerned, for if all hell has broken loose, we'll need to have several vehicles in good working condition in order to survive.

"Sure you can." I glance up to see a little tear in her eye. "Come on, toughen up there. We need you to be able to drive." Her lip starts to quiver. "I realize what happened on Monday, but that was a lifetime ago. We need you to put it out of your mind." I need her to put it out of her mind. "We'll have a lot of *trying things* to do in the near future, so let's get this show on the road." I look down at her plate. "Finish up, and I'll clean up."

Mindy looks down at her plate. "And then we loot the gas station?"

All Gassed Up

I stare at the blood and vomit-soaked seat in the back of the Focus and wonder how to remove it all. There's something final about the stain. A definitive turning point in existence that reminds me of the death of my friend and tells me we are not turning back from this problem. The loss of someone close, irreplaceable, it's almost like the losing one's belief in Santa at a very young age. We still have a lot of daylight to kill in order to do what is needed. All that keeps running through my mind is: the stain will never come out.

Arms encircle me from behind and a warm body presses up against me. I turn and look down into Mindy's dark eyes. Her hair, still a little damp, is plastered to her back. Even without makeup I'm intrigued by her beauty. I'm a lucky guy to have found her.

"I'm ready to go," she says, and releases me from the hug. She tugs at the oversized t-shirt she must have scavenged out of my dresser and I can see she's not wearing a bra again. Call me the luckiest man alive.

"Did you find something to wear besides a t-shirt?"

She smiles and lifts it a little to show oversized shorts. "My belt is keeping them up, but I really need to get some clothes."

I nod. "Where's your place?"

DOUGLAS OWEN

"Markham and Ellesmere, why?" Her eyes widen. "No, we're not going back there."

"Why not?"

"Because I live in an apartment, and if the power is still out we'll need to climb the stairs. Ten floors."

I shrug.

"Remember Frank?" She hooks a thumb toward the back. "We could run into a lot of people like him. Dead and wandering around. How many arrows you got for that thing?"

She has a point. "Okay, but we need to get you some clothes to wear. You can't keep putting bumps in my shirts."

"You don't like my bumps?"

All I see is Admiral Ackbar standing behind me yelling, *it's a trap*. "I didn't say that."

She stretches the t-shirt's neck away from her and looks down. "They're not that big."

I shake my head. This is an encounter I'll not win, no matter what, but something has to be said. "I like your bumps. In fact, I like everything about your bumps."

"Even if they leave bumps in your shirts?"

She's smiling at me, one hand pulling the neck of the shirt down and the other with a finger extended to the edge of her mouth. I'm toast, but there's nothing I can do about it.

"Can we just ignore the stupid white guy and get you some clothes before I run out of anything to wear?"

She nods, still holding the pose. "Sure enough. I guess there's a clothing store in town here…"

There is, but it's one of those recycled clothing stores. Something tells me she'd look good in just about anything, but that doesn't mean I'd make her wear granny clothes.

"Yes, but let's go into Stouffville. There's more to pick from if we can get into a store. Heck, for all we know the world isn't completely screwed like it is in Toronto."

48

It takes a few minutes to pull all the crap out of the car and load in some jerry cans. I make sure all the volatile stuff is secured and stare at the keys in my hand. Should I get Mindy to drive? It lasts a few seconds before I decide not to test her knowledge of standard transmissions, and climb in.

"Ready?" I look over as she fastens the seat belt.

"Ready."

I hit the garage door opener and watch as it rises. Once it clears two feet I can see the street and just about shit.

Lumbering up the sidewalk is a nightmare. Long blond hair, tangled and messy, sits atop a skull with half the flesh pulled off. It's like someone tugged, then gave up once they saw the bone. A limp jaw hangs, telling me it's broken on at least one side. But the worse part is the baby its still trying to nurse cradled in an arm, but to what end I cannot tell. The child also has a face bruised and swollen. The towel wrapped around it is covered with the same purple/green stains that came out of Frank. They're dead. Walking corpses.

The woman's head turns in our direction. Maybe it's attracted by the sound of the garage door opening or the movement. I don't know. All I do know is that it starts to lumber toward us.

Mindy shakes, then her voice rings out clear, "Either drive it over or close the garage door."

I don't know what went through my mind, or why the car started with no complaining when I spin the key. No matter, I spin the key and it turns over. I throw it into gear. My one foot hits the accelerator while the clutch is popped by the other. We leap forward, hitting the garage floor lip and bouncing a little.

The thud against the car is enough to tell me there should be nothing left, but I'm wrong. The woman's head hits the hood and bounces, part of the skull mushed in. She lets go of the kid, who starts to grab at the car. It secures a window wiper and locks both hands around the thing. I want to turn it on. Make it move. Maybe cause the child to let go. But I don't. Why? I don't know why. Something about the stare from those

49

cloudy eyes or something just takes me out of the world and into the unbelievable reality.

We hit the road and I turn south. The heat of the day is just starting to crawl over 36 °C and the car is in no shape to use the air. I look down and see the check engine light flashing, telling me to get it looked at right away. There's nothing I can do now but pray it's just something simple, or we can ditch the car for another. I remember there are a few new car dealerships in Stouffville. Maybe we can grab something there. If the shit has hit Goodwood, then I'm sure it's hit just about everywhere.

Highway 47 is just two houses south of me and there's no traffic, except for a few walking corpses. I ignore them. I ignore the kid hanging onto the window wiper. I ignore the stop sign.

Mindy's voice snaps me back into reality. "Why are you signaling?"

I reach over and flip off the turn signal. "Force of habit."

She laughs. "I didn't know we were picking up another passenger."

The irony of the situation hits me and I smile despite myself. A quick flick turns on the wipers and the kid loses its grip. I do a fast stop and go, making it roll off the hood. Maybe I ran over its head on the way, maybe I didn't. I don't look in the rear view mirror to find out.

The Esso is right there and I turn in, pull into a parking space, and shut off the car. "You waiting in here?"

"You're fucking kidding, right?"

"You have a weapon?"

Mindy holds up a large kitchen knife.

"Guess we'll need to get something for you to fight with as well." I open the door and step out. The day is becoming a scorcher, but at least the humidity is low. Mindy climbs out the other side.

"We getting gas?"

I shrug. "Got lots in the car, but we should fill up the cans." Movement in the store catches my eye. "I want to check out the couple who run the store. Don't want to steal anything just yet." I walk over to the doors, give a little tug, and they open. "Hello, anyone in here?"

A not-so-human sound greets me — a cross between a growl and grumbling in the back of the throat. The same sound Frank made when he clawed his way out of the ground, or at least that's what I imagine.

I find where it is coming from quick enough. A man behind the counter. It's not the owners, just one of their hired hands. He's back there bumping up against the counter top, hands stretched out. Then another, softer sound comes from the sub shop at the front of the building. Must be one of the other workers.

Mindy pushes against me, so I slide out of the way, letting her in.

"Can you deal with the one in the front?" I nock an arrow.

"Depends. Best if you back me up."

I nod, then let loose. The arrow finds its mark. A thud. The corpse is pinned to the back display.

"Nice shot." Mindy hefts the knife. "You'll need to teach me how to do that."

"I think we're going to need more than a bow and knife to keep going in here." I glance about. "They may have a weapon behind the counter. Let's take care of the other one first."

Mindy nods.

The other one is a girl, probably a teenager from down the road. She's behind the counter as well. Mindy tries to stab but only manages to lose the knife while avoiding the clawing hands. I put an arrow through its eye and the corpse is no longer animated.

"I think you're right, we need guns."

"No, we need more bows and a few guns." I gesture to the window.

Mindy turns and freezes. There are several more corpses wandering around outside, most of them across the street. "I don't think we'll be getting gas here any time soon."

I nod. "Maybe we should just grab a few things here and go."

Mindy squishes the bread. "A little hard. Probably everything in here is just about done."

"The freezers may still have cold stuff in them. The cans on the shelves are still good." I hop the counter. "If we take what we can carry,

51

that will stock our supply a little. At least until we can gather some different weapons. I want to be prepared for just about anything."

There's no approval or argument. I look back to see Mindy staring at the ground. "What's up?"

She raises her head, and I can see a tear in the corner of her eye. "I'm useless."

I take a deep breath. "No, you're not."

"Yes, I am." She turns, slumps to the floor. "All I had to do was drive that knife into the thing's head, and you think I could do that?"

I jump the counter again. Kneel down, and place a hand on her shoulder.

"We're going to die, and it'll be my fault."

"No, we're not going to die." I'm wrong, but there's no need to feed her misery. Hell, we could last a few years, maybe ten if we're lucky. "You haven't hunted before, probably never even trained to do any real fighting, so it'll take a while to get good at surviving."

She turns puffy, red eyes toward me and gives a sniffle.

"Now, get up and give me a hand at checking the freezer." I stand, offering the knife and a hand to help her up.

Mindy takes both, though she still is wiping away the tears and sniffling. Going to have to toughen her up. Hell, still have to toughen myself up with all the shit that's going on.

We head into the back. Luck has it there's no one else working in the place. The freezer is still cold, one of those big walk in types. The food's limited, but what's there is still frozen. I close up the door, making a mental note to empty it over the next few days to fill our own supplies.

In the store, I ignore the fridges and head right to the cans and dried food section. I hate this stuff, but it'll last a long time. In an emergency, you'll eat just about anything. We shove two large bags into the back of the car and climb in. We'll need to get everything out of there in the future, before the heat kills whatever's left.

I turn the key and the engine comes to life with minimal complaining. Mindy smiles at me, but it's forced. With a grin I put the

Focus into reverse, take us back, then throw it into first. We have ten minutes to the Smart Centre, and that depends on the traffic.

Traffic is good, besides a few stray cars on the side of the road. I don't even slow down as we pass the police car. Mind you, his vehicle only sticks a little out of the ditch.

The traffic lights don't even blink, so I just slow down a little to make sure nothing comes our way. I've never made the trip so fast, but I stay off Ninth Line and go all the way over to Highway 48 and drive south. We pass Main Street, dodging around the cars littering the intersection. Mindy points out that a few of them have people inside. I slow down and see the faces of death staring back at us. Maybe they stopped and got bitten?

There is no knowing what caused them to die, but a few of the cars have corpses in front of them, legs twisted in painful looking ways. Could have been an accident, bitten, bled out, turned. I suggest not worrying until the way back, maybe putting them out of their misery at that time. She just keeps staring at them as we drive by.

I turn us into the Smart Centre, laughing a little at the Staples store.

"What?" Mindy scans the parking lot.

"Nothing. I was just holding off at upgrading the computer. The new SSD's are in, and Staples has the sole contract for distribution."

She stares at me. "And?"

"Well, no line ups. I can get the upgrade now and not worry about what it'll cost."

She smirks. "Maybe it's a good time to do some Christmas shopping."

"Only 173 days left."

We laugh. It's a good feeling, knowing what we're going through. Anything to lift our spirits.

"I think we should hit Crappy Tire first, see what we need, maybe Wallymart after. That way any food we pick up will be still good."

Mindy smiles. "They have guns in Crappy, don't they?"

"Yes, but not the good ones. We'll have to go into Markham to get those."

"Maybe we can get some sushi?" She starts to laugh.

I grab her hand, give it a little squeeze. "Any time, girl."

We head to the big box outlet. The parking lot is not as crowded, but there are still cars. The solar panels on its roof glint in the sunlight and I make a mental note to scavenge them once the stock in the surrounding stores has been depleted.

No corpses walk about, so I think we're safe. I start to pull up into a parking spot.

"What are you doing?"

I stop, look at the spot. There're five cars between us and the store. Two of them have corpses inside. "It's a good spot."

"Why not park in front of the store?"

I look about. It's not as if someone is going to tow us. "Guess it's just habit." With that, I back up, then drive to the front of the store.

Once the engine is shut off, I get out and look around for anything of danger. "You'll want to take your knife."

Mindy holds the knife up, showing she has it. I reach in and pull out the bow and quiver. A quick movement belts the quiver to my side, not the back like most amateurs do, and take out three arrows. One is nocked right away while I keep the other two in my bow hand, ready to nock when needed.

Shapes move around in the store. I nod to Mindy and she stands at the side of the first door. It opens when I approach, telling me the systems are still operating. I take a step forward and Mindy comes in as well.

The second door opens. The scent of decay hits us both, hard. I almost stumble back while Mindy's eyes water. One of the corpses comes into view and I let loose an arrow. It falls down, fortunately not hitting anything. I knock another.

Mindy whispers, "One down, probably at least another dozen left."

54

I loose another arrow.

"Nice shot," she whispers.

We walk into the place and heads turn toward us. Looks like only a few corpsesare in here. Probably because the doors are still working or something. I shoot down the remaining corpses as Mindy keeps count.

Mindy points to a line of shopping carts. "Do we need one?"

"Probably. Depends on how many things you want to buy." I smile. "Also need to recover my arrows."

"Well, I was just thinking of all the ammo we could get. Also, you could get more arrows if you need them."

I motion to the back of the store with the bow. "Back of the store. We can get maybe a Winchester for you and all the ammo you can carry. More will be in the storage in the back of the store." I try and recall the layout of the shop. "If we prop open the back, we could come and go from there as we like, maybe even block off the way into it so no one will think about it."

"You did."

"Yeah, but most of the people around here are yuppies who moved north to be able to afford a house, and by doing that they drove the prices sky high. Anyone surviving is probably just looking for food."

Mindy raises her eyebrows. "Gotta do what ya gotta do."

We make it to the back of the store and the gun display. There are a few good rifles and one or two hand guns locked in the display case. Mindy raises her knife and I shake my head. "Easy enough to open."

There's a key rack under the counter. I grab it. After a few seconds fiddling, the display opens and I put the items on top for her to see.

Mindy glances up at me. "Which one?"

"Well, the Winchester is a good rifle, and it'll hold this scope." I put a box on the counter. "Also, it's popular so the rounds are easy to come by."

"Rounds?"

"Yes, rounds. Bullets." I put a box of ammunition on the counter.

"Interesting."

I scratch my head. "But the stopping power is not that high with these ones. Mind you, all we need to do is hit them in the head."

Mindy taps a finger against her forehead and looks at me.

"Yeah, something like that." I pull out another box of ammo. "We'll stock up with 180-Grain, it should have enough power to stop just about anything we need it to."

A double click sounds behind me, the unmistakable noise the hammer of a pistol makes when pulled back. I start to turn.

"No, I don't think you want to do that, buddy," a male voice rings out.

Jail House Rock

Mindy stares at something behind me and her eyes widen as cold metal touches the back of my neck. There's no mistaking it, that's a hand gun – large caliber. I race through all the possibilities, remembering everything taught to me in karate classes taken as a child, and each one tells me there isn't much to be done. There's no possibility of knowing if this person is alone or if he has friends hiding out somewhere. And the accent is barely noticeable. Someone from the US, but not of the Southern States.

"Now, I want you to get that girly to put her gun down." The muzzle nudges at my neck. "We don't want anything to happen to you, do we?"

Mindy glances down at the gun in her hand, then back up at me. She hasn't had a chance to load it. And even if she did, what type of shot was she? There's no chance in hell of us getting out of this alive, unless the guy is alone and he used a display model without checking it first.

"You're from the States, right?" I can feel the small dance of sweat beading on my forehead.

"Yeah, just up visiting. So you know I know how to use this." He nudges my neck again. "So get the girly to put the gun down, or she'll be wearing you."

"Mindy, put the gun down, please." I nod just a little.

"Steve, I–"

"Don't worry," I say, mind racing. "I'm sure this gentleman is just trying to protect himself and the people he brought with him."

The man laughed. "Came up here to visit my Pa. You guys locked him up for having a gun to protect himself." I hear him spit. "All hell broke loose up here and now I gotta break him out of the small cell. He's starving in there."

"Your gun, is it from home?"

Pain erupts on the back of my head. I reach back. This is it. The guy's hit me with the butt and I'll black out in a second.

Nothing happens, just pain. I bring my hand back and it's covered in blood. So much for what happens in the movies and TV shows. Guess it takes a lot more to knock someone out.

"Ya got a hard head."

My eyes are watering now. I see Mindy lowering her gun, her lip trembling. I will her to stay calm. Everything's going to be all right.

"Good girly," he says. "Now, take this rope"–a rope is tossed to her from behind me–"and tie your guy up."

I hear him step back as Mindy comes forward.

"Nice an' tight. I'll check once you're done to make sure it is."

I hold my hands out to Mindy.

"Not so fast, smarty. Turn around and put your hands behind ya' back."

A frown tugs at my mouth. So much for that. Mindy is about to cry, but I give her a quick nod and turn to face our captor.

The man, or teen if I judge correctly, stands there dressed in gangster clothes. From the top of his head down to the shoes he wears, total punk. White coat, shirt, and pants. He wears the latter just below crotch level, displaying underwear and what I expect to be a lot of stuffing. Only someone from the Southern States would wear a coat in this weather. The white hat on his head is decorated with rhinestones and tilted with the peak over to the side. His smile widens as I take him in, and there is a flash of a gold grill covering his teeth. He looks partially

58

Hispanic, but I could be wrong.

"That's right, old man, you gotta playa here." He waves the gun, holding it sideways instead of level. He's probably seen a lot of movies. His one arm is decorated with tattoos and I can see the shading of more artwork on his neck. There's a price tag still dangling from the finger guard of the gun. I doubt he even checked it.

"Nice gun." I indicate his weapon. "Found it in the isles?"

His head bobs up and down. "That's right. Found this beast in the display just behind me." His empty hand jerks to the counter behind him. "Let's just say it was already loaded for me."

I know the laws in Canada, and one of them is a weapon on display is never loaded, and the hammer is blocked. He's carrying a prop. The bullets are empty shells only for show. The hammer, if he actually loaded it with real ammo, is made in such a way as to not hit the back of the rounds. And if tried, there's two metal rails blocking, just in case. Safety first, that's what we teach up here.

"So, you fired a gun before?" Tricky, trying to piss him off, but I need him to make the first move. Hopefully what he told me about where he found the gun is the truth.

"You got some mouth on ya." He steps forward.

Mindy's hands stop tying and the knots are still very loose. I unravel one before he's back in front of me, gun pushing against my forehead.

"I should whack you right now. That little girly looks like she needs protection from a real man. Someone like me." His hand is shaking.

"You never killed anyone before, have you?" I gotta push him into pulling the trigger. The shock will bide me enough time.

"Fuck you! I killed plenty this week." He nudges my head with the barrel. "I'm goin' to enjoy killing you."

I can see the sweat on his brow now, smell the stink of his breath. His finger twitches.

"Do it! Show her you're the man!" I push against the barrel.

"No!" Mindy screams.

Too late.

He pulls the trigger.

The distinct click of a dry fire echoes for a moment. He jerks his head, turns the gun a little sideways, and stares at it. This is my chance.

I kick straight at his balls. As hard as I can. He crumples. Drops the gun. I kick again. Same spot. He vomits. Cries. Hands grabbing to try and protect his prize.

Mindy grabs me just before I release another kick on the punk and she is staring at me, eyes red and cheeks wet.

I stop, and she slaps me. Then her small frame is pushing against me, arms circling and trying to crush the wind out of me. Her voice is almost muffled against my chest.

"Don't you ever do something stupid like that again! You hear me?"

The kid is still weeping on the ground, holding his groin. I don't think he'll get up anytime soon.

"I needed him to be off guard." I encircle her with my arms. "That's the only way I could have caught him by surprise."

"And what if the gun had actually gone off? You would have left me here all alone with... with... him." She pulls back a little and her eyes search mine.

"No. He said it, the gun, came from the display. All weapons on display in this store have to be made inoperable. He would need to replace the hammer and remove the bar pins for them to work. And he probably would have removed the tag as well." I glance over at the punk. He's still moaning, but now only one hand is holding his crotch.

"Help me," he lets out, voice all but a whisper and no longer filled with arrogance.

Mindy finally releases me. "What do we do with him?"

I study the man for a second, wondering what we really can do with him. "Maybe tie him up. Take him to the cop shop. Throw him into a cage with his father." The thought goes through my mind of having to come down here at least twice a day to feed the two of them. I dismiss it as something that would endanger us more than save them. "We'd need to take care of them every day. It would hamper us from surviving."

"So what are we going to do?"

I take a deep breath. "The only thing we can do." I step over to the man, flip him onto his back. His bowls must have let go; he stinks. "Toss me the rope."

Mindy grabs the rope and hands it to me.

"Thanks." I take a few minutes and tie both of our attacker's hands together behind his back. "Should hold for the amount of time we need it to."

Mindy has the gun she was looking at in her hands. "So, this is useless because it was on display?"

I nod.

"Where are we going to find weapons then?"

With a finger, I indicate the drawer under the display case. "We just open the place they keep some of the working models."

A groan makes me turn. Our would-be assailant tests his bindings, and then notices me. "Man, I'm hurt. I think you ruptured something."

I gingerly touch my head. The bleeding has stopped, but what is there is still a little damp. I hold out my hand and raise an eyebrow. "And?"

"I was just protecting my own." He rolls a little, groans again, rolls back to his side. "Can't even roll to sit."

The sound of keys, the sliding of a drawer, and an exclamation draws my attention. "Cool!"

Mindy pulls out a box with a picture of a .357 Magnum on it. The Dirty Harry of guns. "Can I have this one?"

"Only if you want to break your wrist the first time you fire it." I look at our captive. "She has a real mean streak."

He shrinks a little.

"I thought the gun would be a little lighter than the box."

A quick glance shows Mindy loading the revolver.

"She's not gon'na shoot me, is she?"

"I don't know."

His eyes widen into saucers and a gleam of sweat starts to form across the brow. There's something about turning the tables on someone who tries to enforce their will on others, or threatens them with death. It shows the character. I squat down, taking the eruption of pain that pushes against my eyes. "And if she doesn't, maybe I will."

There's no way I would follow through with the threat. He's human. Alive. Even though he's the scum of the Earth. Besides, maybe being alive in our new hell will teach him a thing or two.

"I found something we can use!" Mindy shoves a roll of duct tape into my hands. Gorilla, one of the strongest.

The guy struggled against his bonds. "What are ya goin' to do with that?"

I pull a little of the tape free. "Get some peace." A quick tear and a piece is in my hands. I approach and he tries to push away.

"No! Wait! I ha—"

His muffled sound is now little more than a bother.

"Could have waited to find out what that was all about." Mindy pulls back the hammer of the magnum.

Our captive's eyes go wide, then he tucks his chin down and squeezes them shut. The front of his underwear turns a distinct yellow.

"Not such a big man, is he?" Mindy uncocks the gun. "Something tells me we'll need all the ammo we can get."

"We can't just leave him here."

I look around, find the isle with the boating equipment, and snag some of the docking rope. On my return, he's sitting up. His brow is furrowed and eyes squint while trying to balance on one butt cheek. Must have kicked him harder than I thought. "We can use this to lead him around. Not sure about using the car anymore."

We spend just over an hour hunting for the weapons both of us want. I end up picking out a real nice compound bow and two dozen arrows. The tips I grab are razor-edge. The right type for cutting through just about anything. It has a nice weight to it when I pull, and

62

several counterweights to balance the thing out.

Mindy picks up a crossbow, strikes a pose with it that makes my heart skip a little, then laughs.

"It would be better to have a bow." I hold one out similar to mine, but with a little less weight to it.

"Why?" She examines the crossbow. "I thought these were better than a bow."

"Only if you have someplace to duck once you fire." I take the crossbow out of her hands and put the compound in them. "The thing about crossbows is you have to crank it up and then load. The whole process is long when you're looking at a fight or stopping more than one thing. Something tells me we're going to need more than one shot. With a bow, a good shooter can get off two or three shots a second."

"And what about a gun?" She holds up the magnum.

"Good for a short while and has stopping power, but we're not in the movies. If someone gets struck by an arrow, they're going to stop. And the bow makes less noise. You fire that thing and everyone in a few hundred metres will know where you are."

She nods, sticks the gun into her belt and takes the bow. "I can have both, right?"

I reach over and take the gun from her belt. "Only if we can find you a holster."

She laughs. "You really take the fun out of shopping."

We keep gathering weapons until the two shopping carts are full. There's no longer any excuse to stall, knowing our assailant is all alone and tied up with rope and duct tape.

With a little prodding, we get him to stand. He walks slow – with his pants down so low it's almost like walking a penguin. It reminds me of what my friend Phil, an ex-cop in Toronto, laughed about once. Best fashion change he could think of. The perps usually have to hang onto their pants when running, making them either drop their weapon or the goods. And then they're easy to catch, unable to jump or get away.

"We'll take him to the cop shop." I tug at his rope. "Do you have a car here?"

He shakes his bowed head.

"We can find something in the repair bay," Mindy suggests.

I think about it, wondering if there would be anything salvageable in the vehicles left there. "Maybe something that can be used for a quick trip to the dealership."

She smiles. "You're taking me car shopping?"

"Depends on how much you want me to spend." I wink.

"How about a Porsche?"

"How about something good on gas, comfortable, and able to carry what we need?" I start to walk toward the shop.

"You spoil all my fun." She follows, keeping behind the man I lead. "Any smart moves and I'll put an arrow in you."

We make it into the repair area only to see walking corpses in there. Two are dressed in coveralls. The others look to have been customers at one time. All told, I count seven.

Mindy stares out into the bay. "What are we going to do?"

"I could let you have target practice."

She inclines her head and nocks an arrow. At first, she struggles with pulling the bow string, but once it's back to the sweet spot, the last few centimetres are nothing. A little wavering and then the arrow flies, striking one of the coveralls in the shoulder.

"Fuck!"

"You okay?" I glance over.

"The string hit my arm." She switches the bow to her other hand and holds up her arm. The skin is reddish from bow burn.

"Try this." I hold out an arm guard. I fasten it to Mindy's arm. The next three shots strike the same target. Her final, third shot enters the eye and drops it.

"I see what you mean about reloading. A crossbow would be too clumsy."

"Your aim is always a little low." I examine the sights, make a few adjustments. "That should help."

Her next shot hits one of the patrons. The corpse falls.

"Nice shot."

She smiles, bounces a little on the balls of her feet. "See that? Right behind the ear."

"Good shot. Dropped it right away. Guess that's the sweet spot." I drop two in the same number of shots. "Fish in a barrel."

We clean out the rest of the lumbering dead and search for something to hold the three of us and our carts of merchandise. One of the last spots holds a minivan. The work order shows they just finished an oil change. "This is the one."

Mindy frowns. "Rather have the Porsche."

I climb into the van, turn the key, smile at the half tank, and back up. Once out of the spot I drive up to where Mindy stands. "Going my way?"

I get out, and we fill the back with spoils of our shopping spree. Once done, food is all we need, so we push the captive into the back and drive out.

The police station is five blocks away. We pull up, get out, and tug our captive along with us. The door to the station is open, and the shop is empty. Papers are strewn all around, as if people rushed out without thinking of returning. There's an overpowering smell of rot in the air, and I tug at our lead rope to bring the captive with us.

We pass the main desk and swing open the locker to grab the cell keys. Our captive just glares at us.

I tug a little on his rope. "Guess you didn't see them."

Mindy smirks. "Too busy trying to take advantage of people."

We head toward the back rooms, where they keep the arrested people while processing their information. A shudder goes up my back and I push open the door to see the corpse of an old man reaching into another cell where a woman sits cowering in the corner.

Lost Soul

I freeze. The smell in the cell makes my stomach roll. I can't stop staring at the woman. Her short red hair is a mess and makes her mid-thirties age look a lot older. The shorts she wears are covered in dirt smudges as if she's worn them for days. A tattered shirt finishes off the look and red rimmed eyes stare at me with no real acknowledgement.

The spell snaps as Mindy rips the tap off our captive's mouth. "Who is she?"

A smile greets her. "My girl," he responds. "Untie me, Dad needs me."

I clench my fists. There's a desire to hit him. Pummel until my fists are red and bleeding. He is one of the lowest of the low. "Don't untie him."

Mindy slaps him, then grabs the keys off me. She unlocks the girl's cell and steps inside. With slow movements, Mindy starts to crouch.

"Make sure she's not bit." I turn to the man. "Why did you keep her in here?"

"If you don't know why..." He winks.

Mindy is on her knees, trying to calm the girl down. The crying is harsh, and only a few words can be made out, most from Mindy as she sooths the woman.

I grab the man. "I should just put you in with your father."

His grin fades as realization floods his eyes at my meaning.

"You wouldn't."

"Try me."

"Can you do something about that corpse?" Mindy calls out.

I nock an arrow.

"No, you can't! That's my Pa!"

The arrow flies. The body crumples. An arrow quivers in the eye socket.

I turn. The playa's on his knees, sobbing.

Mindy walks the woman out of the cell, glaring at the man as she passes. "Do what you want with him." I swear the room temperature drops a few degrees with her words.

There is no other choice. I grab him by the shirt collar and shove him into the cell. "You can rot in here for all I care."

"You asshole!" He rushes toward the cell door just as I slam it shut. His shoulder hits cold metal bars. The lock holds. "I'll kill you for this!"

I walk away, leaving him spiting profanities and threats to the empty air.

Mindy is not in the main office area, so I make my way outside. She's at the van, helping the girl in. The large eyes of the redhead focus on me and she scrambles into the shelter of the vehicle. Mindy stops and turns. Her gaze falls on me and she shakes her head. I take the hint; the woman is traumatized. There's nothing for me to do but hang back while Mindy climbs into the driver's side. The engine comes to life, and then starts to roll toward me, only to stop a foot away. She rolls down the window.

"Need a ride, sailor?" There's a crooked smile on her lips.

"Sure do, doll." I walk around to the passenger side and open the door.

"I gave her something, just wanted it to kick in." She tosses a box at me. Unisom.

"Never heard of this."

"Basic sedative. Left in the glove compartment. She'll be out for a while, well, long enough for us to get home and tuck her in."

"Any side effects?"

She shakes her head. "No, it's just a basic sleeping pill."

I give a humph. "Well, let's get home before it wears off."

She puts the van in gear, and drives us back the same route.

Crying wakes me from a nap and I toss off the covers, put on pants, shirt, and shuffle off down the hall.

I stop at the door to the spare room and wait. There's small spirts of soothing coming between the light sounds of grief. Not wanting to eavesdrop, I head down the stairs to the basement to pull out something for dinner. Frozen lasagna, perfect comfort food. I head for the kitchen, turn on the stove, and set it for 425 °F. As it heats up, I unpack the frozen slab, remove the foil, and sprinkle more cheese on it. Into the oven it goes. 90 minutes. I go upstairs, into my office, and pull up the file I use to record what's happened…

Strong hands squeeze my shoulders, waking me from slumber.

"Did I fall asleep?"

Mindy kisses my neck. "You sure did. What's this?"

I go to close the file. "Nothing much."

"My name is there. Let me see."

I pull my hand back, stand up, and motion for Mindy to sit. She obliges, and starts to read. There's a lot of information recorded in the documents I've stored to keep track of what's happened to us, and it begins with what started our hell on Monday. I go downstairs, letting her read the file.

The lasagna is just about ready when Mindy comes down to join me.

"So, I'm the hot Asian chick you're referring to in the journal, am I?" There's a crocked smile on her face.

"You sure are."

She stands there, looking me up and down. Her playful expression starts to melt and she pulls her hair away from those beautiful eyes. "We should cold shower this for a few days."

"What?" Here comes the shocker. She's going to say goodbye to me. Something I expected to happen last Tuesday, but didn't come for some reason.

"For Jill." She pulls out a chair and sits. "She's been through a lot. That son-of-a-bitch raped her every time he went to see his corpse father." Her shoulders slump. "Maybe if she just sees us being good to each other it'll bring her around. We've been a little sleazy of late and, well, that's not really what I'm like, most of the time."

"Most of the time?"

"Yeah." She takes a deep breath. "Normally I'm one of those straight-laced people, but sometimes I just lose control of myself and, well, hitch up with the guy I want. It's been a while since I've felt something for anyone, or believed I meant more than just a quick lay for someone." She glances up. "Until I met you."

Two steps takes me in front of her and I kneel. "I've never met someone like you, either." I take her hand. "If you think it'll help, I'll do it."

Her smile brightens my existence, and makes me very happy I'm a man. I stand, lean forward, and kiss her with soft tenderness.

The oven buzzer goes off, breaking the spell. "Dinner will be ready in five."

Jill joins us for dinner, but her eyes dart to me all throughout the meal. The arched eyebrows tell me everything I need to know – she's still traumatized. And for Mindy, I keep my conversation to a minimum.

69

Not that there's much to say. We eat mostly in silence. Only a few words come out of Jill while we sit. And most of those are stilted, to the point, and leave nothing to chance.

I make sure she has lots to eat, though she doesn't take the plate from me, but waits for Mindy to pass it to her. So I just sit and shovel food into my mouth.

Once the two women eat their fill, I collect the dishes, and take them to the sink. Jill uses that to excuse herself, and makes a dash to the stairs. A door slams.

I return to the table and sit down. "That went well."

"What do you expect?" Mindy collects the last of the lasagna. "She spent a week in that cell being raped by that guy, and the times he wasn't raping her, that corpse tried to get at her."

The idiot feeling comes over me. I should be more understanding. The woman went through hell before we found her. "How long do you think she'll be like that?"

Mindy puts the tray on the counter. "Who knows?" She comes back to the table, sits down. "She could recover in a day or a month. Heck, it may take a year, or never."

"What can we do?"

"Just be understanding, patient, and try to be helpful, just like you usually are."

I understand the instructions. Just be normal. Understanding. Patient. Walk on egg shells. Guess I could do that.

Samantha jumps on the bed, lands on my bladder. She lets out a whimpering whine to tell me know she's hungry. I think about the bathroom while the light of the pre-dawn dances on the leaves of the tree outside my bedroom window.

"I think she wants food," Mindy says as she rolls over, one leg entwining mine. "Maybe you should get up and feed her."

"Maybe you should." I reach over and tickle the little spot on

70

Mindy's side that I discovered a few weeks ago. She squeals, leg twitching. Samantha pounces on it by kicking off me. The pressure makes my bladder scream. "Okay, I'll get up."

The covers come off, I reach for my pants and pull them on. Before I exit the room, I give Mindy another tickle.

"Better get me a coffee for that."

I just laugh, heading for the bathroom.

Nothing sets the mood for the day like a good morning pee, so that's what I do. Then off to the kitchen, Samantha trudging down the stairs before me.

The light is on in the kitchen, and I wonder if it was even turned off last night, but I'm sure of it. Not for the first time I wonder if there should be an automatic shut off for the rooms facing the street. I didn't expect to see Jill there, a coffee in her hand, sitting at the table.

"Morning," I say, trying to be as non-confrontational as possible. To my surprise she glances up.

"Morning," she replies with a soft voice.

Best response I've had from her since we found her two months ago. "Do you need anything? I could make breakfast…"

She looks down at Samantha who is wrapping herself around the woman's legs, purring so loud I'm surprised the windows aren't shaking.

"I think you'd better feed the cat." She stands up, walks over to the counter stool. The coffee cup comes up to her lips and she sips. "How long?"

I stoop to pick up the cat dish. "Excuse me?"

She sips her coffee again. "How long since you two picked me up." The words came out more like a whisper than anything else.

The question takes me aback. We picked her up on July 9th, now it's September 15th. I play is safe. "Just under three months."

The cup comes back up to her lips, then stops. "What happened to him?"

I need to be careful. Something, anything, can tip her back over the other way. "He won't be bothering you again."

71

She takes a sip, then puts the cup down. "I need to know." A deep rumbling breath goes through her body. "What happened to him?"

I put a scoop of food in the dish. Samantha rushes over, sits up and waits.

"I've never seen a cat sit up before," Jill says.

"She picked it up from Charlotte, my last cat." I put the dish down, stroke Samantha a little, then straighten up. "I locked him in the cell you had."

She stares at her coffee cup. I wait for her to comment.

"So, he could still be alive."

"I don't think so." I reach into the cupboard, take out two cups. "Who would let a criminal out of a jail cell?"

"You did." She gulps the last of her coffee.

What can I say to that? "It's not like you killed someone."

"No, not killed." She gets up, walks to the coffee maker, and pours some into her cup. "At least, I hope not."

"What happened?" I put the cups down beside hers and she fills them.

"A guy tried to pick me up at the bar."

She puts the coffee urn back on the burner. There's still some left, so I don't tell her to turn it off. The coffee releases a strong aroma, so I open one of my containers and throw some sugar into it, then powdered whitener. I notice the jar is almost empty and make a mental note to bring some up from downstairs.

Jill sits back on the stool, sips the black tar. "I was drunk, so was he." Her voice sounds hollow, no fluctuation. "I told him I wasn't interested, but that didn't stop his groping. Finally, I just laid in on him. Just kept hitting him even after he fell. I guess someone saw it and called the cops. Next thing I knew they threw me in the drunk tank to cool off. That's when everything went to shit." Her shoulders slump together. "That's when they put that shitty old man beside me. And everyone left." Her eyes gloss over for a second. "Then that guy came in. Sonny. I don't know if that was his name or just what his father called him."

"How did the old man turn?"

"He was bitten by some kid before he came into the bar. Guess that's what set him off." She shivers. "Never saw anything like that. He puked, cried. Finally, after a night, died, and came back the next morning." She gulps more coffee. "He came in the next day, saw what happened, had keys…" Tears well in her eyes.

"You don't have to say anything else." I cross my arms. "You went through a lot."

She puts both hands between her legs and shivers. "No, I need to tell someone. Mindy's nice, but young. Sonny first gave me some water. Must have had something in it. Next thing I know is he's on top of me. My shorts off, and the father reaching through the bars at us. He was fast, at least. But he smelled foul. Never gave me much rest. Kept showing up and sticking me."

I uncross my arms, shove hands in pockets.

She motions to the cups. "You better take that up to Mindy before it gets cold."

"Do you want me to come back down?"

She stares at her hands for a second. "No, enjoy your morning with her. I know I've put a little damper on things for you over the last while. I'll be okay, Samantha will keep me company."

I can just see Samantha's head poking over the counter. She's sitting on the stool next to Jill, examining the counter top. Probably looking to see if there's any more food for her. I grab the two cups.

"We'll talk later."

She nods as I make my way upstairs.

Mindy sits up as I enter the room. She's wrapped a little shawl around her shoulders, but it's not that cold.

"What took you so long?" She reaches out for the cup.

"Jill was downstairs."

Her eyebrows rise. "And she stayed there while you made coffee?"

I hand over a cup, the one with only sugar. "Nope, she had it made when I went down."

Mindy almost spills her coffee. "Really?" She takes a sip, makes a face. "That's strong. What did she say?"

The thought goes through my mind about how much to tell her. If Jill didn't tell her anything, then who am I to break the confidence she placed in me? No, Mindy should know. I don't want to keep secrets from her. Not at this stage in our relationship. So I tell her everything Jill told me about what happened. I didn't keep anything out. Spilled it all. Mindy just listens, nods, sighs, gives a small whistle, and finally says, "And how did she seem?"

I sip at my coffee. "Lost."

Mindy gets it, she really does. For all the crap she talks about, there is a kinship between women when it comes to sex, and if they've been violated… It's why fathers keep a loaded shotgun by the door when their daughters get picked up on a first date.

"You're lucky." She takes another sip.

"What do you mean?"

Mindy puts the cup down. "I tried talking to her about it a few times, but I guess she wasn't ready. You talk to her for the first time and she opens up to you."

I climb into bed.

"Then there's all the times she disappeared upstairs when you came around, like she was scared of you or something."

I reach over, put an arm around her.

"So, when you come up and tell me you had a decent conversation with her, well, that just about tips the scales."

I kiss her side, not on the part that's ticklish.

"I don't know what it is about you and people willing to talk to you."

"I don't think that's fair." I place a hand on her stomach. "You've only seen me with one other person, and I locked him away."

"And put a gag on his mouth."

"And walked him to the vehicle all tied up."

She sighs, and I can feel myself getting excited.

"What are you doing?" Mindy lifts the covers a little. "Oh! Good morning."

"Yes, it is."

The fire alarm beeps out in panic, pulling me out of the euphoria of our lovemaking. I jump out of bed, causing Mindy to roll over and almost out of bed as well. The pants go on quick, as the thoughts of all that noise attracting those we don't want to bring to the house. I head for the stairs, pull the alarm, wave it about until the noise turns off, and toss it to the side.

The blur of stairs pass under my feet as the smell of burning bacon fills my nostrils. Once at the bottom, I see my skillet on the counter, a pack of frozen bacon sitting on it, smoke rolling up. I pull the plug and hurry around the counter to see Jill sitting on the ground, crying.

I dump the bacon in the sink, and run the water.

Once the smoke stops, I turn to Jill and sit down beside her. She curls up in my arms, balling. I let her stay there, getting it all out.

Soon, the sobbing stops, and she has left streaks of tears down the front of my shirt. Mindy comes down the stairs, she sees us and I wave her back, still worried about what will happen if I let Jill go.

There's a silent agreement between Mindy and I, something we both understand. Jill needs someone to cry on. A shoulder that is not angry, questioning, or demanding of answers. So I give it to her. Let the fear, frustration, and angst come out. It takes a while, but soon she pulls away.

Her hand wipes at the tears streaking down her cheeks.

"Sorry, I don't know what got into me."

Once lost, now found.

Rolling Thunder

The lights flicker on and I take the last two steps into the basement. I've kept the heat down as the cold November wind batters against the house. Most of the leaves have changed and dropped to the ground, leaving skeleton fingers stretching to the sky in a morbid tone for the year. We now have to be more careful with what lights are turned on, for there's nothing covering the front of the home from possible prying eyes.

Jill follows me into the basement. Although closer to my age than Mindy, she's more a sister-type of person. We joke every day while the three of us play cards, but she goes to bed alone, and most of the time crying. My heart goes out every time I hear the weeping at night, but there's nothing I can do.

The basement is just that, a poured concrete floor a little over two metres tall. Enough to use while standing up, but not enough to make any real living space. Storage is great, as long as you keep everything to one side. I'd hate to have the septic break over food or something.

Every month I count out our food and other supplies. Every month I figure out what is needed. Every month I worry about where the stock is going to come from. This is the second time counting this month. It shows how much I worry about our future, now with three people surviving off what I scavenge.

Mindy accompanies me to the stores and we pile cans of food into the cart. We both keep our bows with us, shooting any corpses that wander by. Lately though, I've noticed signs of someone else using the stores, telling me we're not alone anymore. It's hard to tell, but last month I marked the top corner of a bag of sugar and a few cans of stew. We'll see if they're still there when we hit the stores again today.

Wood is piled in the garage for winter. I think we cut enough. Thank God for the high efficiency wood burning insert. I still remember the salesman wondering why I wanted wood instead of gas. "It's better than paying someone for the fuel when I can just cut down a tree and grow another one in its place. Renewable energy, that's the future of our race." Go figure how true that is today. If I took the gas fireplace, well, we'd be freezing this winter. Geothermal is good, but the shorter days means less solar power, and the system does take a bit of juice to run. Burning wood in the fireplace adds so much to the heat in the house.

Jill reaches out and touches my arm. "Where are you?"

I snap back into awareness. Letting my mind wander is not a good thing. "Sorry, just thinking about the fireplace. Think we have enough wood?"

She smirks. "Let's see. You said it burns about three logs a day to help heat the house, winter is really the only time we need it, but it is nice to have it going today. Say about 120 days. That means about 360 logs, give or take. You piled up about fifty logs in the garage and another 500 in the back, so I think we're good. What do you think?"

There's always been a fear I'd never have enough. A gripping hand always on my stomach telling me I should save that extra serving instead of eating it. When Dad passed away I was only sixteen. Mom worked, but we never really had enough to keep us going. She pulled double shifts, paid the mortgage, bills, and we ate what we found on sale. There were always interesting ways in which she made meals, like peas and toast, potato soup, and a whole bunk of other stuff. Things I call comfort food. Guess that's why I built the lauder in the basement, why I always bought bacon when it was on sale and stockpiled it in the freezer, why canned goods line the basement wall. All we need now are eggs.

Jill thumps my arm. "You're doing it again."

"Sorry, just thinking about what we need."

"Eggs, milk, cheese. Shit like that."

"What about beer?"

Her eyes gloss over for a second. "A good stout."

"Thought that would bring back memories."

She walks over to the work bench, examines what I have there. "Have you ever thought of brewing your own beer?"

"Not really. Actually hate the stuff. I'm not a bitters type of person."

"Hence the reason for the lack of it in here."

"Cat's out of the bag."

"So, what's your poison?" She picks up a hammer, gives it a few swings at the air, then puts it down.

"I like dark spiced rums, some liquor, a few other things. Basically, the sweet stuff." I count out the canned ham, only four left.

"What you say we hit the liquor store today?"

The thought had never crossed my mind. Liquor is, was, so expensive in Canada that I thought of it as a luxury item. "I think you've got a good idea."

"Maybe we can use that new truck you picked up. The plow may help move some of the crap off the road." She picks up my circular saw, frowns, then puts it back. "We could also pick up some lumber, see if we could build a little shed out back, put a still or brewery in it…"

It's the first hint of her actual plan, and it's not a bad one. "So, who's going to be the brew master?"

She puts down my drill. "That obvious?"

I laugh, then frown as I see we only have one can of corned beef. "Just a little."

"Should I be a little more up front?"

"Probably would help." No more cream corn.

She walks over. "Do you think anyone else survived?"

I stop counting the canned beans. It's a good question. Is there anyone else around? We've made a trip into both Uxbridge and Stouffville just about every week to stock up. Heck, even picked up one of those huge curved big screen TVs for us to watch movies and shows on. Never thought much about looking for people.

"I think there are people around. If they keep out of the way of corpses." We see them most of the time. The lumbering dead don't move very fast, but they never sleep. I always take different routes in order not to draw their attention to the house. It hits me that we should pick up some snowmobiles soon, that way we can move around in the winter with greater ease. Heck, I'll even leave them my Visa so someone can charge it.

"Maybe we could find some?"

I stop counting again. It's that question. Find some. People always have baggage. A person can be the nicest one you've met one minute, then a raving lunatic the next. There is no telling which people are out there, or if they want to be found, contacted, bothered. I imagine what it would have been like in the early part of last century, before the wars, when the small area we live in held a total population of 30. Everyone knew everybody. But then again, a great deal more space separated the homes, no internet, only a few had telephones, and TV was unheard of. A time when communities did things together. Need a tree cut, ask your neighbour to help out. Now, I'm worried about what is in my neighbour's home.

Jill waves a hand in front of my face. "Does that mean yes?"

Reality comes crashing back on me. I put down my notepad. "We can see if anyone is interested, yes." My mind races through different scenarios on what could happen. We find another group, all of them named Sonny. They kill me and rape the two girls. Suddenly, I don't really want to find anyone anymore.

"We'll need to be careful. Something like using radios in order to talk to people first, then maybe meet on common ground with no way to trace back to the house if they turn out to be…" Fuck, I almost say rapists. With all that Jill has been through, reminding her of it is not something I want to do.

"You mean like Sonny." She puts a finger on one of the shelves. "We should see if they have any cookies at the store as well."

"I'm sorry."

"About what? We need some condensed milk as well. Mindy is using that in her coffee. Oh, we should really stock up on that as well."

"About that."

"Condensed milk?"

"No, for having that lead to pulling up the past."

She just stares at me. A slow tremor crosses her lower lip. Eyes start to brim with tears. Then, suddenly, she is back to normal. "Nothing happened to me."

Denial. There it is. This is how she's moved past everything. Shoved it all into a neat little room and locked it away, never to look at it again. This is what they call the unhealthy part of surviving, supressing it until, one day, it explodes and makes a mess of your mind. I'm not trained in how to work this out. One thing is for certain, we need to find someone for her to talk to.

We stand outside the Walmart door in Uxbridge, and because it's on the outskirts of town, I think it's the best one to go to. I'm nervous about how many people used to live in the core, and how many corpses would be walking around. So far, the small stores have sufficed, but their stock is almost gone.

We take my new truck, a liberated GMC pickup super-crew with extended box. Probably worth around $90,000. No problem, I borrowed the money from the bank and left it on the sales manager's desk. Picked up the truck just from the dealership a week ago. No one complained when I drove it off the lot. Even put a dealer plate on it, making Mindy laugh. Took a few days to put the plow on, but it works. Getting good with this mechanical stuff, even without YouTube.

I picked out the diesel, knowing the fuel will be easier to come by and does not degrade as fast as regular gasoline. There's little to worry about except oil changes. And if it breaks down, I can always take it back to the dealer. Even picked up a brochure for the extended warranty. Mindy laughed when she found that in the glove box. Told her better safe than sorry.

We all piled in, drove to the Walmart, and now here we stand, staring at the doors. I've never been in it since the corpses started to walk. Wanted to, but not sure what to expect. How many are in there? Is there anyone else inside? Are they friendly? Just a few of the things I worry about every day.

And then there's what will happen if we do find someone. What do we do if they want to come back with us? How do we keep them, and us, alive? Another one of those questions that's better not asked when you're looking for other survivors.

Mindy holds her bow, quiver at her side; I've got my compound, quiver also at my side. Jill has copied us, but she also has a backpack. We designated her as the carrier, since this was her idea.

Jill looks over at me. "Think the doors are locked?"

"Don't know." I take a tentative step forward.

Mindy grabs my arm. "Shouldn't we get ready, you know, just in case?"

"Oh, right." I pull out three arrows. One gets nocked and the other two I hold in my bow hand. "You ready?"

Mindy nods, holding her bow at the ready. I see she has the hammer pulled back on the glock at her waist, safety on. Something I really didn't want us to need, but guns are a good backup if you run out of arrows and have something walking toward you wanting to take a bite.

Jill steps up beside me. "Let's get some radios."

We step up to the doors, stop, frown.

Mindy laughs. "So, I bet they don't even have a greeter here either."

I shake my head, step up to the door, try to slide it aside. To my surprise, it moves freely, allowing us to enter the first section. Very little light streams into the place, and I know we'll need to be careful if anything is lurking inside.

"Everyone ready?" I flick on the lamp strapped to my forehead and get ready to slide the final doors open.

Jill and Mindy switch their lights on as well, nock arrows, and nod.

This door does not move as easily. I put my weight into it and finally it moves, letting the stale air fill my lungs. I cough, catching the odor of rotten meat and fungus-filled bread.

"Let's go," Mindy says as she steps forward.

I walk in, letting the doors close behind me. "Stay together. Three sets of eyes are better than one."

We walk into the store, head lamps moving like flood lights in front of us. They're good camping lights, spreading out in a decent arc before us, but nothing beats full sunlight.

Jill glances to the ceiling. "I thought all these stores were supposed to have solar panels."

"Corpses don't fly," I say. "Keep your eyes in front."

We planned out what to do. First, get to the electronics area. Second, find some long range radios. Third, pick up some canned goods. Fourth, get the hell out. The hope was there would be no corpses, no people, just us getting what we wanted and moving on.

Mindy releases an arrow, nocks another one quick. A corpse hits the ground.

"To your left," I tell Jill. She aims, lets loose. Another corpse topples to the ground.

Jill nocks an arrow. "See any more?"

I let an arrow loose, making another corpse drop. "Not moving."

We continue, find seven more, each dispatched with ease.

I keep scanning the distance. "This is too easy."

Mindy lets loose another arrow. "Want it to be harder?"

Jill coughs. "Bite your tongue."

Another eight go down. "I don't think we're going grocery shopping any time soon," I say.

Mindy let's another arrow fly. "I need condensed milk, and I think we're almost out of coffee."

"Shit," Jill says. "Steve, we need coffee. I've seen what she's like if she doesn't get her fix. Not pretty. I also need naps."

I groan. "Why do woman always ask the guy to pick up the feminine products for them? Do you know how emasculating that is?"

The girls let out a quick laugh, stop for a second, both let an arrow fly. "Double header," Jill announces.

We're three metres from the electronics area. I spy a corpse standing by the counter, milky eyes turn to stare at me. It starts to move its whole body, bumps into the counter, and topples over, bashing its head against the ground. It fails to stir.

"Doesn't count," Mindy says.

"Right you are," Jill responds. "No arrow or bullet, no joy."

"How's your quivers?" I count mine, still have over a dozen.

"Fine," Mindy says.

"About seven left." Jill lets go an arrow. "Six."

"Shit." We didn't expect this many in the store. Not a good sign. We each started with two dozen. "Make each one count. Guns when we all run out."

The corpses seem to be either to the left or right. None along the path we're taking to get to what we need.

At the counter, I see the radio area and we walk closer to it. "I don't like this. We're bottlenecked in here."

I grab two of the same packages, stuff them into Jill's backpack.

"Time to go, ladies!"

We have no real plan for escape, just run for the exit, don't trip. Jill moves fast. Her legs pump against the ground like running thunder. Mindy keeps up with me. A few of the corpses try to follow but they're slow. I estimate nothing more than a lumbering walk of three or four kilometres an hour. As long as we don't get hurt or overrun, there's no reason for us to fear them, unless you count the horror of watching a corpse lumber after you, mouth open, puss running out, skin hanging off bones. Yeah, nothing to worry about.

Jill hits the doors, struggles to pull them apart. It gives me the chance to catch up. I try and help, but for some reason the doors won't budge.

"Pull!" Mindy cries out.

"We're trying," Jill grunts out.

"Something's wrong." I stop pulling, check the points where the two doors come together. I can see the metal lock joining the two. "Fuck! It's locked!"

Jill jumps to the other door. She pulls, and nothing happens. I quickly check the door as well. A realization comes over me as I hear Mindy's voice. "I'm switching to the glock."

Thunder erupts from the pistol.

"How the fuck did this happen?" Jill kicks the door.

"There's no way they locked by themselves." I hammer at the door with my bow. "Crap, not sure what type of glass that is."

Two blasts echo in the building. "Hurry up guys, the crowd is getting ugly."

"Fuck! Let me out of here!" Jill hammers her fists against the door. A degree of hysteria creeps into her voice. The thought of being locked up must be running through her mind, bring to the surface what she went through before we found her.

Mindy fires another three rounds. "They're attracted by the sounds!"

"Stand back," I tell Jill.

She pulls back, wiping spittle and tears from a red face.

I pull out my glock and fire into the door. The rounds puncture the glass, making finger fractures spread out. I kick at the spider web, sending shards of small safety glass at our feet. A quick run of my bow along the frame scatters what is left of the glass. "Let's go! Move!"

We all hit the next doors and find them locked as well. "Fucking great day," I say.

Not wasting time, I aim the glock and pull the trigger, letting the shots go up the door. A quick kick sends the glass tumbling to the ground just like the other door.

We run for the truck. I pull open the drive's side and jump in. Mindy and Jill do the same on the passenger side. The nice thing about a new truck isn't the new truck smell, it's that it'll start on a dime. The engine turns over just as a corpse erupts from the building. I slam the truck into gear, and hit the gas.

The power of an oversized diesel engine throws us back into our seats and I steer us toward the exit, and the line of Harley motorcycles that block it.

Hell on Wheels

I bring the truck to a stop. There's eight single headlights blazing in front of us and several corpses shambling out of the doors of Walmart behind. One of the bikers unslings a rifle and starts shooting at the dead escaping the store. His shots find their mark as I realize he's using an automatic rifle. Totally illegal in Canada, but who's going to tell him that? At least none of the shots are aimed at us.

On the largest bike sits one of the biggest men I've ever seen. His long gray beard is braided into two ropes that reach to the middle of his chest. The helmet he wears is more a brain bucket than anything else, and the spike on top glints in the sunlight. His leather jacket shows signs of the road, and is undone to reveal a black t-shirt with writing that I cannot make out at this distance. Chaps and cowboy boots, both black, complete his look.

The biker guns his engine, then shuts it off, allowing for a little backfire to split the air. He swings a leg off and lets the beast of a bike rest against the stand, then pulls off his helmet. Gray hair spills down over his shoulders, and he stands there with his arms crossed.

"What the fuck is he waiting for?" Mindy whispers.

I reach down, take out my glock, prime it, and place the weapon on my lap. "Don't know, but try not to show him we have any guns."

Jill is shaking beside Mindy, who puts her arm around the back of my seat.

The man starts to walk toward us, unslinging an assault rifle, carrying it cradled in his arms. He stops a few paces in front of us, staring through bushy brows, before shaking his head and coming up to my window. The stare he gives me takes a few years off my life. It's a hard stare, like Gandalf confronting a small hobbit. He reaches out, and taps the window softly, making a circular motion with a finger.

I hit the window control and it slides down into the door.

Nothing. He just keeps staring at me. Then, a deep rumbling sound escapes his lips. "You new here?"

The sound of his voice takes me back, and I glance at Mindy, then Jill, before turning back to him. "Actually, no. How about you?"

The corner of his beard twitches. "Not many people would go into a store like that, unless they're looking for something in particular."

I swallow, let the sweat roll down my back. "Just needed a few things, you know, to help get by."

He reaches into his jacket, pulls out a short, thick cigar, and a zippo. The latter he strikes, and applies the flame to the stogy's end. He puffs it to life, closes the zippo, takes the cigar out of his mouth, and lets out a stream of smoke at the end of the stogie that makes it glow with intensity. "We've been here a while and not seen your truck before. Where you holding up?"

"Just outside of town," I lie. "Nice little farm house away from everything."

His head goes up and down very slightly. "We've checked out every place within five klicks of the town and not found anyone." He takes a long pull on the cigar, rolls the smoke in his mouth, then lets it out. "Where about's are you?"

"Concession four, north of Wagg, near the gun club. Our house is tucked behind the trees." I try to remember the area as best as possible. "Driveway kind'a looks like a dirt road."

He nods again. "We thought there was nothing in this area."

Jill takes that time to speak. "Nothing? There's got to be other people here."

I can see his smile through the beard.

"Nope. We checked every house. Nothing but these walking corpses." Another shot echoes, making us jump. The biker doesn't even flinch. "We claimed the town a few days ago. Didn't you see the signs?"

I run the road through my head. There were no signs. "No, didn't see anything." I swallow. "If we're trespassing on what you've claimed, I'm really sorry. We'll leave and not come back."

He puts the cigar back into his mouth, the end flairs as hot as the sun for a few seconds. "I take it you picked up some stuff from our Walleymart there."

"Nothing much, just a few talkies. Too busy staying alive." I reach over and grab one of the radios, hold it up. The scowl on his face grabs my bowels and squeezes.

"I figure those, that being in our Walleymart, are ours."

Another shot echoes through the air.

"We can trade for them," I suggest.

His eyes move a little, gaze landing first on Mindy, then Jill. "What you have for trade?"

"Not much," I say. "I can get some stuff from home and come back with it for you."

His eyes narrow, focus coming back to me. "Got any weed?"

"Sorry, I don't have—"

"We need weed, cigarettes, cigars. That's what we'll trade for what is ours."

"I can get some," Jill says. She reaches down, comes up with a map. Didn't know she had one. "There's a dispensary just two towns over. Little messy probably, filled with corpses."

"Didn't see no dispensary when I went through Stouffville." His brow furrows. "You wouldn't be pulling my chain now, would you? We could use some girls." The smile comes back to his face. "Our guys would like a girl, and you have two."

There's no way I'm going to give him one of the girls, not for anything. "Sorry, Min's my wife and Jillie here is my brother's wife. We can't give them up."

He takes the cigar out of his mouth, blows out a lot of smoke. His other hand comes up and scratches the back of his neck. "Well, I'm sure one of the guys wouldn't mind you then."

"Sorry, not interested." Even if hell freezes over.

"Then I recon we have a problem here." He takes a step back. "You broke into our store, took merchandise, didn't pay for it or ask permission, and now you don't have anything to trade."

Even in the cold, sweat beads on my forehead.

"We'll take the truck." He motions with his hand for us to get out.

My balls seem to grow and I'm done talking to this man. He seems to think the world is his, probably would follow us back to the house and take what he wants; raping Mindy and Jill, probably even me, just out of spite.

I shake my head. "Don't think so." My right hand lifts, showing him the glock I have pointed at his chest. "I think we'll just drive on out of here. We'll not come back, and you don't try to follow us."

He smiles wide, teeth holding the cigar. A light chuckle escapes him. "What you going to do with that pea shooter?"

I squeeze the trigger. The kickback is slight, but the noise loud. The shot hits him high in the shoulder, driving him back. I slam on the accelerator, barrel right toward the bikes that block our path. The rifle guy squeezes off two shots, but we have the blade on the front and it catches them both. Bikers jump out of the way, leaving their rides behind. Then we hit gray beard's bike. It crumples and spills from the plow. Three of the bikes are out of plow range. The rest are shattered. Bikers rush to them and jump on.

"Try to take them out!" I yell.

Mindy climbs into the back, opens the sliding window, and fires off three shots. "I'm out!"

I toss my glock back at her. She grabs it and starts firing again. Three bikers follow us, their headlights weaving in my rear view mirror. The others take pot shots at us just behind them.

Jill pulls out her gun and rolls down the window. "Thanks"

"For what?" I really want to know.

"For not treating me like property and trading me."

"Never crossed my mind." I turn onto Highway 47. "Now, take at least one of them out, will you."

She leans out the passenger window and fires a couple of rounds. I see a bike skid a little, then topple.

"Nice shot," Mindy says, and one of her rounds takes out another. "Easier to shoot when you steady your aim."

Searing pain erupts in my left shoulder. A red hot poker of fire finds its way into my body. I fight to keep the truck on the road.

"Oh shit!" Mindy screams. "Steve!"

I grit my teeth, hoping the round went through me and was not lodged inside my body. Since the pain is only bursting the back of my shoulder, I'm sure it didn't go all the way through. Fuck, so this is what's going to kill me.

"Are they still following us?" My voice is calm, but I can feel myself losing against the pure shock of what happened. I keep both hands on the wheel. White knuckles point forward like beacons.

"No, the last one stopped after his buddy went down." Mindy pushes me forward a little, her fingers probe the searing pain. "Get us home."

I roll into the garage, fighting with everything to stay awake. Darkness narrows my vision. Everything sounds as if kilometres away. I don't know if I'm pressing the gas or break, but we come to a stop before the back wall and Mindy hits the remote to close the door. Everything fades to black.

A voice echoes in the distance and all I can see is darkness. Fingers probe at my back shoulder, then the pain returns with added fire.

"Steve, we have to get the bullet out."

"Mindy?"

"I'm here, Steve. Stay still, this is going to hurt."

Coolness touches part of my shoulder, then it hits a point, driving pain through my body. Icy hot needles jab at the bullet hole and the world goes dark once again.

The heat of the fireplace warms my feet. Mindy is there, and so is Jill. I watch as children run around the house, playing good guys and bad. Mindy says something but I can't hear her. She smiles, and motions for someone to come over.

An old man enters my view. His short cropped hair is all white, and the top of his head shines in the firelight. He says a few things and nods, but I cannot make the words out.

Mindy places a hand on my cheek, kisses my forehead, and a jab hits my right shoulder.

I wake up, groggy at first, but the pain reminds me of what happened. Voices are talking in the kitchen. A kid's face comes into view, brown eyes and scruffy hair. He smiles, showing missing front teeth, then disappears from sight.

The stamping of feet drifts to me, then Mindy's face is in front of me. She smiles, then kisses me. My mouth tastes like shit and I desperately want to brush my teeth before she does it, but she seems to not mind.

Jill is there, I can hear her voice. She's talking to someone, asking questions. I can make out what is being said, but it sounds like nonsense to me. Something about a bullet wound. Yes, that's right. I was shot.

"How long?" My voice sounds horse.

"A week." Mindy smooths back my hair. "You've been in and out for a week."

"I pulled the bullet out." A man's voice this time. Something very familiar about it. "I'm not sure how your shoulder blade isn't shattered, but for some reason it stopped there."

"Probably because the bullet had to go through the truck and seat before hitting him," Jill says.

I turn my head and she is sitting in a chair beside me. "Hi," I say.

"Hi. Glad you're not dead." She winks.

"Me too."

"We owe you a lot, Doc," Mindy says, and then it hits me. Doc. The animal clinic. It's Doc Parsons. I took Samantha to him for her shots.

"Don't worry about it." He comes into view, bald head and gray hair. He smiles with those blue eyes. "Steve's a good guy. He always takes care of his animals and pays the bill without much grumbling." He puts a hand on my forehead. "Temp seems right, but if his nose gets warm…"

Jill laughs. "We'll bring him in for shots."

Doc laughs as well. "Right." His hand touches my good shoulder. "Take it easy, Steve. I'll be back in a week to see how you are and to remove the staples."

"Thanks, Doc."

"Now get some more sleep, the girls have everything under control." He smiles, then winks.

"I'll see you out," Jill says, and gets up from her chair.

"Thank you," Doc says.

They both head to the kitchen.

Mindy still strokes my hair. "You need a shower."

"And a toothbrush."

"You're telling me."

I start pushing myself up but use my right arm. Pain erupts in my shoulder. Mindy reaches out and pushes me gently back onto the pull out bed.

"You stay put, doctor's orders."

I let myself back down. "What happened?"

Mindy takes a deep breath. "You got hit by a lucky shot from one of those bikers." She stands. "I'll get a cup of warm water and your toothbrush."

She walks to the bathroom. Water runs, the cabinet opens. She returns with a cup and my desperately needed toothbrush. They're put on the side table, and Mindy comes to my left side and helps prop me up.

"Better?"

"Yes, thanks."

She hands me the cup, then goes into the kitchen, returning with a bowl. "Just spit into this."

I nod. She already put toothpaste on the brush so I proceed to make my mouth more female friendly.

"You got us home just before passing out." She sits beside me. "Jill said she saw an ad for a vet clinic just north of us, and she took the truck out to it. When she got back, Doc was with her." She held the bowl while I spat out foam, then rinsed.

"Doc was nice, remembered you fondly." She took the bowl into the kitchen, then came back without it. "He's a vet, but knows his stuff. I helped him, you know, all that drilling to be a doctor and all. He pulled out the bullet, stapled you up, then dressed the wound." She placed her hand on mine. "There was something on the bullet that infected your shoulder and he had to reopen you the next day and debride it before closing it up and pumping you with anti-biotics. He works well on people." She stoked the hair out of my eyes.

"Did you know there's a bunch of people just north of us who are still alive? Jill wants to get together with them on their next meeting, see what it's all about. Doc says they're trying to secure the area against roaming gangs and the walking corpses."

"Does he know what's causing the corpses to come alive again?"

"No, but he's been in touch with someone in the city by radio. Says he's with the Public Health Agency. They've been trying to figure it out."

"Guess that means they don't know either."

Mindy sighs. "No, they don't. It's reached all of North America and we're cut off from the rest of the world." She stares off into the distance. "Darlington went cold."

No wonder the power went out. Darlington supplies most of the electricity for the area. "What about hydro-electric like Niagara?"

"No idea."

"We have all those wind and solar farms, at least some of them should be feeding the grid."

"Doc says most of them are feeding the communities around them. You know, the ones who complained about them years ago. It seems very few people decked their home out like you did, solar and power wall storage."

"I did it to save on utilities. Money left to me by Mom when she…" I don't want to finish the sentence.

"Well, regardless, most places have a lights out curfew a little after dark. Not many people know how to generate enough power to sustain their own needs, let alone share some with their neighbours." She kisses me again. "I've missed you."

The admission that I was missed hits home. It seems like Mindy and I are a couple. Me, the geek from the computer room, dating the hot Asian chick. Who would have thought?

The door to the outside opens. "You two decent?"

Mindy laughs. "No, but our clothes are still on. At least mine are."

Jill walks into the front room. She holds a small bag. "Doc gave me more bandages for pin cushion here. Says to keep him off his feet for a couple of days. Plenty of water and sleep. He can start having soup tonight, maybe even sooner if he's hungry."

"Hello, I am in the room."

"Did he say anything else?"

94

Jill sits on the other side of the bed. "Yeah, the gang in Uxbridge is getting worse. They've raided a few of the outlying communities and have been taking people, girls mostly. Young ones, but a few of the older ones as well. Usually, they kill the men unless they can think of something to do with them." A shiver runs through her. "Some are used for sport."

"Maybe they're trying to build an army," I say.

"Could be," Mindy says. "But if they are, why take the men who were close to the women they take?"

I shake my head. "Easy. They hold them and tell the poor guys to fight or they take it out on their wife or daughter. Easiest ploy there is."

"What are they doing about it?" Mindy stands, walks over to the kitchen.

"They want to clear them out." Jill takes my chin, moves my head from side to side, gives a grunt, and stands. "They want to raid the gun club's firing range and gather up all the weapons, but no one knows where the group stored all the ammo and rifles. It's something of a mystery, and all the signs for the gun club are down, so the gang isn't going to find it any time soon."

"I think—"

"There has to be someone familiar with the gun club still alive." The whine of a can opener broadcasts something and Samantha scurries out from under the bed.

"We can try—"

Jill gives me a look. "There're lots of things people can try, but not knowing the layout of the club means we'll be in there with a lot of people. If the bikers happen to drive by, they'll see the commotion and come in force before anyone is ready."

"I know where the rifles are!" I finally blurt out.

"What!" Mindy and Jill both say at the same time.

"I laid out their computer network and they showed me around. Including their storage and where the keys are."

A Stupid Plan

One week lying in bed is difficult, especially with two watch-dog women keeping an eye on you. Every time I want to do something, one of them would appear to either help or just do it. Sponge baths are only fun for the first couple of times, then the one giving them starts to have the fun and you're helpless.

I do manage to start moving around with a little pain after the third day, and now, just a day before Doc is scheduled to come by, getting out of bed is easier. My appetite is back, and Mindy kids me about putting on too much weight if I keep eating the way I am. They keep me full of water, and the times they go out, I sneak some of the flavour crystals I like into it. Who cares if they say those chemicals cause cancer.

Now I just wait, Samantha laying on her back using me to balance. I'm just lightly scratching her side, the way she likes.

The rumbling of the garage door opening sounds throughout the house and I know Mindy and Jill are back. They are the only ones with the opener so it limits who's coming in.

Samantha flips to a more lady like position, feet under her, but remains laying beside me. Her ears twitch, locating the noise and focusing on it. The garage door closes, and the outside door opens to the two women in my life talking and laughing. Something I don't hear very often.

Mindy is the one leading their parade into the house, both are carrying cloth shopping bags.

"Well, look who's being pampered now." Mindy bends over and taps her hands together. "Come here, Samantha."

The cat springs from her spot, jumps off the bed, and saunters over to Mindy as if it's her idea.

"What a traitor." I cross my arms, pout a little. "Just come home and take my cat away from me."

"Could be worse," Jill says. "She almost picked up a dog on the way home." She puts her bag on the counter. "But it was really skinny and snarled when she put her hand out."

"I got something for you, girl." Mindy pulls out a tin from her bag. "Time for yummies!"

There's the sound of a tin lid being pulled off, and I'm truly shocked that she found tuna or something for Samantha. Jill stares at me, smiling.

"We found the storage area for the pet food shop." She pulls a bag of dry kibble out. "Sam's not going hungry for a while."

"We also ran into one of the people from the small community north of us." Mindy comes to the counter, puts down a tin. "They have a meeting tonight about what to do for security."

"Okay." So, my brain appears to be working right. "What are we going to do about that?"

"Duh, we're going." Jill points back and forth between the two of them.

"I'm going with you."

"No." Mindy comes around the counter and toward the bed. "You're staying right here where you'll recover from that gun shot."

"I'm okay. Heck, Doc will be here tomorrow to remove the staples."

"And until he does, you're staying where nothing can cause them to rip out." Mindy motions with both hands for me to sit up.

"They're healed." Even with my objections, Mindy pulls up my shirt and examines the wound.

"Not only did you get shot, but something got into the wound and put you out of it for a while. That's why I want you to be safe." Her fingers probe gently. "Anyway, there's still a scab on the thing and I want it fully healed before you start moving about."

"Come on, I'm going crazy just laying here." I swing my legs over the side of the pullout. "I tell you, I'm fine." A big breath, hold, push off, and stand. My legs stay under me. I let the breath out. "See?"

Jill comes around the counter. "He does look like he can stand."

"It's not the standing I'm worried about." Mindy gets off the bed, walks over to face me. "Lift your arm."

I left my right arm into the air. There's a tug at the staples, but other than that, nothing.

"Asshole. Lift your left arm."

Crap. Okay, going to have to do it. I left my left arm, slow. At 45°, my back tells me to stop. Muscles complain, but nothing I can't ignore. At 90°, the staples in my back scream. It's like they were put through the skin and into the bone beneath. Sweat starts to bead on my forehead and I try not to grit my teeth.

"Stop," Mindy says.

I keep pushing. 100°. I stop, hold my arm there. If I find the guy using plyers to pull at my back I'll kill him.

"Pain?" Mindy puts a hand on my chest.

"Yes." I don't lie. She knows me now and can tell if I do. Anyway, she probably feels the thudding of my heart and tension of straining muscles.

"Put it down."

I lower my arm. "I'm still going."

"No, you're not ready."

"You leave without me and I'll follow you."

She takes a deep breath, stares at me for what seems like an eternity. Those dark eyes hammer away at my abilities and I'm just about ready to relent.

"Okay, but I'm driving."

Jill smirks. "Great."

Mindy turns to Jill. "What?"

"One can't shoot and the other can't drive. I'll take us there."

Jill jumps into the driver's seat, leaving Mindy and me to decide who's going to be shotgun. I let her have it and crawl into the back. We're all wearing dark clothes and I notice the plow is sporting a new, black, paint job as well as some specialized lights.

"Night lights," Jill says. "Not so much bright, but they light stuff up good." She hits the remote and the garage door lifts up. "The bikers have a new game they play – called find the car."

"Find the car?" The name confuses me.

"Yeah, they drive around at night trying to find someone out and about. When they do they toss these on the road." She reaches into the glove compartment, pulls out something, and tosses it to me. "I think they call them caltrops."

The metal contraption is interesting. Four nails joined in the centre, with their points in different directions. I lay it flat on my hand and one point is facing up. A quick turn and another point is up. Very similar to the old caltrops used in the middle ages to stop horses, but more effective for tires.

"No matter how they land, a point is always up." Jill backs the truck out of the garage. "Makes it hard to keep your tires intact."

"I can imagine."

Mindy smiles. "Yeah. When you're approaching them, they toss them on the ground. The plow usually handles them, but I put it down and the guy didn't think I'd swerve into him."

"Is that why the plow is painted?"

Mindy just smiles a little, looks at the roof. "Maybe."

Two killers, that's who I live with. "Maybe we should hold off on all the outings you two have been doing. It's not a good idea to be taking them down so close to the house."

"Oh, we're not that—"

"Mindy!" Jill turns to her. "Enough. Steve needs to know what this meeting is about."

"Sorry. I just got a little excited about all the stuff we found in town."

"You didn't go to Uxbridge again?" Dread rises in my gut.

"No, Ballantrae. Lots of stuff there if you know where to look." Jill throws the truck into gear and taps the garage remote. We all watch as the door closes. "Down. Time to go."

She hits the gas and the back end spins a little on the fresh snow before the tires grip.

Jill slows down before Sandiford Road and engages the left turn signal. Mindy giggles.

"Sorry, habit."

We turn onto a dirt road with several tire tracks. Jill travels along the path as if she's been on it a number of times. A farm house, hidden behind a number of trees, comes into view. There's a dozen other vehicles parked in front, ranging from trucks to a few sports cars. Seems someone did a little shopping during the police absence.

Jill pulls up beside a truck with huge exhaust pipes reaching into the air behind the cab. I recognize it, the vehicle with no muffler that kept me awake the first few weeks after I moved into the house.

I turn to Mindy. "Do we know who's going to be here?"

"Doc didn't say." Mindy opens her door.

"This ought to be fun." I get out.

"Time to meet the group." Jill opens her door as well.

We walk up to the front. Jill reaches out and rings the doorbell. Nothing happens.

"No power." I reach out and knock on the door. Jill stares at me

100

with vacant eyes, then it hits her and she rolls them.

There are a number of things to do when waiting for someone to answer a door. I reach over, take Mindy's hand, and give it a squeeze. She squeezes back, leans her head on my shoulder.

Through the frosted glass, a light bobs toward us, and after a few seconds, the door opens a crack, stretching the chain holding it. One wrinkled eye scans us up and down. There's a mop of curly gray hair atop the head.

Jill leans forward. "We're here for the meeting. Doc told us."

The door closes, then opens all the way. An older woman stands, staring at us. "And who are you?"

"Steve from Goodwood." I point first to one woman then the other. "Mindy, and Jill. They stay with me."

"Humph, Schitts Creek Steve." She motions for us to enter. "Come on in. My name's Cindy. Welcome to my home." Cindy looks behind us. "You can relax, Bill."

The sound of a hammer being eased back fills the empty air. I glance around to see a shadow figure in a ghillie suit wave and disappear into the night.

Mindy swallows. Jill has her hand on the gun in her belt.

"Don't worry, he only kills when I tell him to. He's a good son." Cindy beckons us in.

We enter. Cindy locks the door then heads through the hall, and downstairs to the basement. As we hit the landing, she reaches across, flips a switch, and a five metre square room lights up.

Cindy turns to us. "Welcome to the security meeting."

Cindy introduces us to the group, naming everyone sitting around the room. I only remember a few names, like Doc and asshole Carl with the loud truck.

Being stupid, I decide to confront him about noise pollution. "How do you keep the corpses off you with your truck making all that noise?"

Carl pulls off his baseball cap, runs fingers through his thinning hair. "Had ta bypass the system. The stacks were just to lessen the back pressure during racing. I closed it off and now the truck is all but silent."

Good reason why we don't hear him anymore. "Guess that's why the cops never stopped you before."

"Oh, they stopped me. But because the bypass was in place, they couldn't do a damn thing about it. Takes corpses to do that."

Cindy steps forward, claps her hands three times. "Looks like we're all here. So, Doc, why did you call us all up?"

Doc stands, glances around the room, then motions to Mindy, Jill, and myself. "Well, as you know, there are a lot of bikers in Uxbridge right now, being led by some guy they call Pa."

A shiver runs down my spine. That's what Sonny called the corpse in the jail cell.

"Well, he's starting to expand the area they claim." He pulls a folding map out of his back pocket, looks around for someplace to put it.

"Here, we'll tack it to the wall." Cindy reaches for it.

With the map secured on the wall, Doc continues, "They've claimed from Davis to Wagg, and Concession 4 to Marsh. This is what they seem to patrol all the time." He taps the intersection just south of where I live. "Soon, probably in the next month, they'll claim out to this area." Doc looks right at me.

"And maybe up as high as this." He points to Sandiford road. That gets some of the people to squirm.

Mindy stares at him. "What does this mean?"

"Well, Mindy, it means they'll overrun your home. Take you from Steve, probably kill him, and put you to work on your back for their guys." Doc gives her a hard look.

"I won't let that happen," I say. "Hell, they can try, we'll just find another place—"

"With solar panels and power wall storage?" Mindy grabs my hand. "The house is the reason we've lived so comfortably over the last while. Can you imagine finding another one just like it someplace?"

"Even the clinic doesn't have that type of setup," Doc says.

Carl cleans his fingernails. "I have something similar, but it works off wet cells. I figure you have less power loss than I do and a heck of a lot less panels on your roof."

Cindy nods in agreement. "Our system went up ten years ago and I have more loss then you have. I got 30 panels tracking the sun during the day."

"What everyone is trying to tell you, Steve, is that we're probably the best off of the bunch." Jill puts her hand on my shoulder. "Even with the limitations. The wall is full power usually by two and I've never seen us use more than 50% of the stored power."

"Wait until winter," I say, remembering the time I even went up on the roof to clean the panels.

"Regardless of that, we have to figure out some way to tell the bikers they have to stay out of our area." Doc sits back down. "They come in, kill the men and rape the women. Sometimes they take the kids as well. Both boys and girls. I'd hate to think of what they do to them."

"Indoctrination." Jill stands. "They need to keep replacing the riders they lose to the corpses, or someone who fights back." She glances at me. "The gang is called Family, and Pappy is the son-of-a-bitch I whaled on before I got thrown into jail."

I don't know what to say. Jill, the one we rescued from Sonny, knows the guy who runs the biker gang. Everyone starts talking at once. Carl stands up, voice raised. I can see his face redden as spittle drips from his mouth. Doc is quiet, too quiet. One hand is messaging his chin. Cindy is ghost white, probably wondering who she let into the house. Others argue back and forth about what to do with the person who could be a biker sitting in their midst. Me, I'm just wondering how the hell to survive.

"Jill"–I grab her arm–"you said you almost killed him."

"Just about did," she says. "He wanted to have sex that night and his grimy hands fell on me." She glances away. "I didn't ride with them for long. Was thinking of leaving after Stouffville, but we ended up in the bar with a few too many drinks in us."

Mindy looks at Jill. "How did you get mixed up with them?"

"Usual thing. Getting away from an abusive relationship, needed to get someplace far away, they were the only ones heading south." She sighs. "Good life choices, right?"

Doc stands, puts two fingers in his mouth and whistles. Everyone quiets down.

"Look, so she knows the bikers, so do a lot of you. How many times have we encountered them and survived? Eh? Carl, you've had the most experience with them. Does that mean you're a member of their ranks?"

"Hell no, they keep stealing gas off me. Lucky I got enough to run the truck."

"And William, how about you? I know they visit your farm all the time."

"Gotta make fries for them when they show up or they'll shoot the cows." He wipes his eyes. "One raped my daughter."

Doc lowers his eyes. "Sorry, you didn't tell me that." He takes a deep breath. "But we've all suffered from the hands of these people. Even now, I bet they're trying to figure out where one of us lives in order to get something they want. Basically, we have to protect ourselves, for no one else will with the way it's going now. There's no law, no police, and probably no military unless they're all in Toronto trying to protect that hole."

Cindy recovers. "So, what do we do?"

"We need to come up with a plan to arm ourselves in order to survive. When winter hits fully, they'll want more of our food and fuel in order to survive, and believe me, they don't care one bit about our needs or wants."

Everyone in the room nods.

"If we were in the States, each of us would have a gun," Carl comments.

"And they would have more than they have now," I say. "Look, the gun club is close by. Why not raid their stock and arm ourselves that way?"

"Because their guns are hidden somewhere." Carl runs a hand through his hair. "Besides, it's in their zone of control."

"Not really," I say. "They control up to Concession 4. The shooting club is west of that."

"The driveway into the place is still off Concession 4." Carl puts his hat on.

"Yes, but if we use the Lafarge pits off of Concession 3, we could get right on the property without any problems." I stand, walk over to the map, and point.

"And what then, smart ass? How do we find weapons none of us has ever seen?"

Mindy smiles. "Because he's seen where they keep them."

Doc lets the talking carry on for almost a minute before he lets another whistle go and levels his eyes on me. "How do you know where the guns are kept?"

"I rewired their network last year. They wanted a closed circuit video feed and a secured server network controlling it. So they called me."

Carl lets out a barking laugh. "And you're some type of computer geek?"

"Actually, he is," Mindy says. "You should see the setup he has at home. An IP server and media boxes, flat screens, and a stereo, all controlled by his remote."

She plays it up a little more, but I just stand there, blushing as she names off all my toys.

"Okay, can you draw us a map of their club house, Steve?" Doc hands me some paper and a pencil.

"Probably, but I was only in there a couple days."

"More than any of us."

I sit down and start sketching from memory what comes up. Most is the data lines I put through impossibly tight holes. They insisted nothing more than three millimetres be used. Probably because they sealed all the holes once I left.

"Here you go, the vault"–I point to one wall–"is right inside this room."

Carl smiles. "Great, rocket scientist knows where the vault is. So what's the combo?"

"44-23-88-90," I say with a smile.

Yippe

Jill stops the truck just outside of the ATV shop in Stouffville. We get out and she pulls a bow from the back seat. She scans the street for anything that breaks the morning silence.

I step up to the front doors and give a pull. Locked, just like I thought. Metal grates decorate the back and front of the glass door, so breaking it is not a solution. Besides, the door's not big enough to let us get anything of worth out of the dealership. I check the fence and it's not locked.

A quick tug opens the gate and I walk through at a leisurely pace.

There are crates stacked in the yard of various shapes and sizes. I pull my coat tighter as a brisk wind whips through. There are just a few things to look for and a lot of stuff to grab your attention.

I hear the truck engine roar to life and red washes against the ground as Jill backs the big vehicle into the yard. She stops at the trailers, gets out, and grabs her bow. An arrow is nocked right away. She's being safe.

Not worrying about what's behind me, I turn a curious eye to several ATVs. One looks brand new but I can tell the hell it went through due to the cracked front cowling and oil on the ground. I need to get one that is used, but not killed. If we can find two or three, that would make our day.

Another door leads to the showroom. Just what I wanted, and when I test it, the thing's not locked. I pull, and the smell almost knocks me on my ass. There has to be at least one corpse inside, and it's ripe.

I give a low whistle and Jill looks up. She comes over and the wrinkling of her nose tells me she hates me. I'll still need at least two weeks before I can hold a bow properly, and another to practice up to the level needed to be of any good. Rust begets rust.

Jill steps in and I unclip my small flashlight. One flick ignites a slim beam and I use it to scan the area. Nothing. No corpses so no danger from what I can see.

"I don't like it," Jill whispers.

"Neither do I." I level the beam to the back of the showroom and see exactly what we're looking for. Two quads, camo paint job, and ready to go. They have tags on them, showing the things were newly purchased, meaning the pre-delivery inspection was done and they are ready to hit the ground running. "See what I see?"

"We need those." Jill steps forward in a crouch. She keeps the bow ready to fire and I follow her in. One step at a time.

She stops. "Did you hear that?"

"No."

"I thought I heard one of *them*."

"Nothing." I step beside her. "I don't see anything. Maybe it's in the shop."

"I don't care where it is. Let's get the bikes and get out of here."

Jill's right. The best thing we could do is just get the hell out of the place. Let the corpse be a corpse and do corpsey things the way corpses do corpsey things. The living need to live. Anyway, if there's more than one like the Walleymart incident...

I squat walk to the first bike. Keys are in it. The battery is disconnected. Don't need it yet. I slide it into neutral, give it a push, and it rolls easy enough. There's a roll up door in the front so I manoeuver it that way, between stacks of merchandize and stock. Jill is right behind me with the other.

We get to the roll up door, a big corrugated metal thing, and I pull the latches on either side. "Get the trailer and truck. Once you bring it around, I'll start them and we can load them up."

"Right." Jill slinks back the way we came.

I check her bike, battery is disconnected as well. With a little work, I get them re-attached. We're ready to roll.

The truck pulls up and I grab the bar holding the chain for the roll up door and tug it out. A quick pull of a chain and up it goes with a ratcheting sound, making me cringe. Sound carries in winter, especially in the cold air.

I return to the bikes and jump on the first one. A turn of the key brings the machine to life. I press the start. Gears whine as the long dormant engine tries to start, then catches. The quad fires up and puffs out smoke with a roar. In gear it goes. Up the ramp. Onto the trailer. Motor off. Brakes on.

I head back to jump on the second one.

Movement on the distant street alerts me to corpses walking around. I stop to examine the actual numbers. A group of over twenty are coming across Main Street from downtown.

"We need to hurry!" Jill whispers in a not so quiet voice.

I nod, move to the other bike, and climb onto it. This one doesn't light up when I turn the key. It doesn't respond when I push the start. Nothing happens.

"Come on!" Jill calls out.

"Fuck you," I tell the bike and jump off.

"What are you doing?"

"The fucking battery is dead." I scan with the flashlight, looking for a battery. Any battery. None are out. "Fuck. I bet they're in the back."

"We don't have time for this." Jill comes into the showroom. "We'll push it."

"Up the ramp?" My shoulder is already screaming at me.

"Got a better idea that'll take less time?" She starts pushing the bike. It moves a little at first, then speeds up. When it hits the ramp, she manages to get the front tires half a metre up before they start to slip down. "Give me a fucking hand, will you."

Even though bikes are not heavy, they are cumbersome to move around when not under power. The wheels are knobby and stubborn. Almost as stubborn as Mindy but I convinced her to stay at home while we got the bikes. She's getting the guns ready for tonight.

I put my back into it, and together we push the bike up and onto the trailer right behind its mate. Jill and I make quick work fastening it down. We practiced a bit on the lawn mower but something tells me this isn't Jill's first rodeo.

The last strap is tight and tested. Jill jumps behind the wheel and I take the passenger seat.

"Go!" I yell.

Corpses jostle toward us, attracted by the sound. I estimate their speed and how fast we can get around the corner. We'll be hard pressed to make a perfect run for it. But we have to try. She slams the truck into gear just as the first of the small group of corpses round the drive and they get the plow. Jill lets out a "Yippe" as their heads impact the solid blade, which now has teeth welded on the top. She likes doing that too much.

Mindy greets us at the door, Samantha in her arms.

"How did it go?"

"Not bad." I take off my coat, hang it in the hall.

"Cluster fuck at the end," Jill says. She throws her coat at the wall pegs. "Let me see your back."

"I'm all right."

"No, you're not. Let me see your back."

I lift up my shirt. Jill pokes at it for a second, then pulls it down.

"You need to see Doc tomorrow. I think those staples either need to come out or you have another infection."

"What? Let me see," Mindy says and puts Samantha down before pulling up my shift.

"Damn, can you two just let me get in the house?"

Jill grabs my arm. "We both care about you. Not for the same reason. I'm not spreading if that's what that look is for. It's just that… well… we take care of each other. You and Mindy are like siblings to me. If anything happened to you…"

There's something in her voice. I take her hand.

"I've never had anyone in my life who didn't either want to get in my pants or take advantage of me in some way. You two both have done nothing but help me from the time you got me away…" She wiped tears from her eyes. "Shit. Look what I'm doing now."

Jill stomps into the front room and up the stairs. The door of her room slams shut.

"She's right," Mindy says.

"About what? Not wanting to fuck her?"

Mindy's fingers stop probing. "You really can be an asshole when you try." She pulls down my shirt. "You'll be okay. It's not an infection, just… the staples need to come out."

"I can drive up to Doc's place today."

"*We* can drive up to Doc's place today," Mindy corrects. "We're supposed to keep an eye on you."

"I don't think I'm going anywhere very fast."

Doc cuts the last of the staples out of my back and lets out a humph. His hands still move quick for an old guy and I can barely feel the alcohol hitting where the hole and cut had been.

"You healed up nicely," Doc says.

"Chalk it up to clean air and good sex," Mindy says.

"Kids." Doc hands me back my shirt and faces Mindy. "And how are you feeling today?"

"I'm good. No more sickness." Mindy jumps up on the exam table beside me. "Not sure if I'm eating right, though."

Doc puts a blood pressure cuff on her. He's decked his office out a lot different in the last few months. More human medical equipment than anything decorates the place. "And what about your appetite? Any increase or cravings?"

"Not really, does that mean something?" Mindy takes my hand.

It hits me. I glance up at Doc who is wearing a big grin, then at Mindy, who's giggling. "Are you…"

She breaks out into a laugh.

"We're going to be…"

Lips kiss me.

"Pregnant?"

"Yes, you big dink."

"But how?"

Doc shakes his head, puts his hands in his pockets, and starts to walk out of the room. "And they called my generation slow."

Mindy's still giggling as I pull into the garage. She answers the questions but leaves a lot to be interpreted. And when I enter the house, Jill is there with most of the group, all smiling and happy. Even Carl has a grin on his face.

"So, how'd he take it?" Jill asks.

"Not bad." Mindy hangs up her coat.

"You knew?"

Cindy comes over from the kitchen. "I could tell when I saw her the first time. My question is, what did you think the little lump on her tummy was?"

I take Mindy into my arms, give her a hug. "Guess this makes it official."

"Not yet. We still have to get married." Mindy gives me one of those long stares with squinted eyes. Her smile just brightens up my life.

"Who said anything about marriage?" I think for a second, trying to find out when I said anything about it, or if I did. "We don't even know

112

if there's a priest still alive."

"Oh, there's a priest all right," Cindy says. "He lives just in Ballantrae, like Doc does."

I try to remember where the church is in that area, but fail. There are so many more survivors than I knew about. They keep themselves hidden, just like us, until they are needed. It kind of helps renew my faith in the world.

"Well, we'll have to figure something out after we get rid of the bikers."

"About that, did you get the quads?" Carl asks.

"Sure did," Jill says. "Just need to test them out and gas 'em up."

Carl smiles. "I should have gone instead of you, Dad."

I shake my head. "No, Carl, you don't send in a big gun when a small pistol will do." I reach over, put an arm around Jill. "Besides, I had the best partner anyone could ever have with me." I lean over and give Jill a kiss on the cheek.

"Yuck! You're so gross." She squirms out from under my arm.

Carl laughs at our antics. "Can you show me what you picked up?"

"Sure, but first I want to make sure everyone has something to–"

"I'll be delighted to show you what we got this morning," Jill says.

I glance at her and she brings the corners of her mouth up the slightest amount to show a smile. Jill and Carl. Hell, poor guy probably doesn't know what he's getting himself into.

"Well, looks like there's a little party here tonight. Want to join me?" I hold out my arm to Mindy.

"Don't mind if I do, sir."

I have the map spread on the dining room table. Not a big map, but a local topical one for the area. Jill and Carl are back from their little bout of show and tell while Mindy has not left my side. I've marked my... our, I correct myself, house on the map and the basic route to take to the gun club.

"One thing you should know, the Lafarge pits are old, so they could be deep." I put a finger on the north pit. "They've been on this pit for a good twenty years by now. And since it's back a bit, we could be looking at major flooding from the fall rains."

"Don't worry about the pits," Carl says. "I've been in there a couple of times and they didn't dig as deep as most people think."

I look up from the map. "When did you go in them last?"

"Just before the shit hit the fan." He pulls out his wallet, digs out a card, and tosses it on the table. "Driver 33 reporting for duty."

That's why I didn't like him. "So, you were a dump truck driver?"

"Yes, but I tried to get the town to open up Wagg Road for traffic. That town council was bought out by someone who wanted no trucks on Wagg. Probably one of the rich home owners. Not sure, but you know the woman who represents us?"

"Yeah, well, no. Never met her. Busy working."

"Well, it turns out she was one of the members who always voted down opening Wagg and closing Concession 3 south of the last pit for trucks." He picked up the card, stuffing it back into his pocket. "Someone had her in their pocket. Dirty politics at any level will always be dirty politics."

"Thanks for letting me know." I put my finger on the map. "Since you know a little more about the area inside the pit, why not fill us in?"

Carl steps forward, starts to tell us about the gravel crusher and where they kept it. He explains how steep the wall of the dig is, and where the best parts for running the bikes should be. Finally, he ends up by telling us the fence is missing on the north side. "No kids up there."

The plan is coming together, and I feel confident about the map drawn earlier. I spread it out, looking again at the crooked lines and childish hand writing. Cursive, wish they taught it in school.

"The clubhouse is just the front of their operation. We'll find some rifles, but the ones we want are kept in the vault here." I tap a small building on the map I drew out. "Most of their automatic weapons are stored behind a barred area. It reminds me of a police lock up area for

114

their guns." I flip the map over, showing an inside overview of the building. "We can get to the basic stuff from this area, but all the ammo is in the safe in the basement." I tap the map again. "We get into that, and we'll have ammo for a long time to come. We just have to remember to close if up after we're done."

Carl scratches his head. "Why?"

"Because if we don't and the bikers find it, they'll have all the ammo they need." I flip the drawing back over.

Carl stares at the map, puts a hand in his back pocket. "Why don't we just take all the ammo out with us on the first trip?"

"Two reasons." I hold up one finger. "First, they have a lot of ammo. More than we can hope to haul away with two quads." I hold up another finger. "Second, who would store it? Can we keep it at your house?" His eyes start to light up, then he squints with one at me. "Thought not." I take a deep breath. "It's best to take just what we need for a month, split it up so everyone has enough, and come back for more later on. What do you think?"

Doc pats me on the right shoulder. "Sounds like a well thought out plan."

Carl crosses his arms. "I guess I'm in."

Cindy nods. "Me too."

The rest follow Cindy's lead, saying they would like to go as well.

"We only have two quads. And even though some of you may have one as well, we need to keep it small and fast. That way, if anything happens, we'll be able to get out in time before any shit hits the fan." I look at Doc. "You're staying back. We don't have anyone else with the training you have so it kind'a makes you indispensable." I turn to Cindy. "I know you're a strong woman, but being the leader of the group means no risks." Jill is staring at me, arms crossed. "I doubt if I could keep you off the team even if I ordered you not to go."

"Damn straight," she says.

"Okay, that means me, Carl, Jill, and one other."

The young kid, not more than sixteen, gets out of the chair he used to watch the meeting. "Count me in as well."

I struggle to remember the kid, but don't. "What's your name?"

"Call me Billy."

Wrong Number

I look over to the clock. 4:42. it's time to get moving, before the sun goes down and darkness envelopes the area. That way we can get to the gun club without using headlights. We don't want to announce our arrival to anyone while we go in and raid the place. Not very elegant, but the utilitarian in me likes it.

Jill walks over to me with Carl following her. She goes over to the bike that wouldn't start when we picked it up yesterday morning and looks it over.

"Is it starting now?" She turns the key.

"Yes, just a dead battery."

She taps the start and the small engine turns over. "Good to see the tank is full. You have a small trailer for it, right?"

"Two, actually. I decided to use the one Jill is playing with, that way if there's anything really wrong with it, I'm the one who'll be hiking in the dark. You two want to give me a hand?"

"Sure," Carl says. He walks toward the back of the garage. "I take it they're out back?

I give a nod and Carl goes out to take a look.

Jill keeps fawning over the quad and I come up beside her. "You know what you're doing?"

"Not really."

"The back brake is on the right foot, right thumb is the accelerator, left handle the front."

"You're an ass, Steve."

I glance at the ground. "Honestly, he seems to be okay now, but before he was a real ass about making as much noise as possible with his trucks." I see a small tag on the bike, start to peel it off. "How much have you two talked?"

She stands up, places hands on hips. "Not much." There's hesitation in her voice. "He lives out of town on a wooded lot. Not much to do but cut down trees, hunt, raise babies."

"I was thinking—"

The back door opens. I glance over my shoulder and Carl is coming back in. "We'll talk later." With a quick squeeze of her shoulder, I stand. "They look okay?"

Carl removes his hat, scratches his head. "Okay, I guess. One has a tire that's a little low on air, but other than that, they should hold a couple hundred kilos each."

"Good." I turn my attention to the hitches on the back of the bikes. "We should get them hooked up. It's about time for our little raid."

A shiver runs through my body as the cold wind out of the North West finds even the smallest opening. Carl is driving the other quad and is a good ten metres in front of me. Jill rides behind him, arms wrapped around his body. I don't know what to think about that but she's a grown woman, and I'm not her father.

The kid, Billy, hangs onto the back of my quad, doing his best not to touch me from his perch on the seat. Hell, I'm a stranger he's only met today, so who can blame him. He only had a heavy sweater on, so Mindy gave him her leather coat. I swear he almost recoiled when it touched him.

We pass Wagg and the sun starts to hit the horizon to our left. Once it's down we'll need to be inside the gun club, or risk being seen with our lights on. So far, no one's seen us. Thank God for small miracles.

Carl flashes his break lights, slows down. I pull up beside him and lift my visor. His is already up.

"Looks like the gate is locked." He motions to the swing gate in front of the pit's access road. "There's a key in a box on the side, but if that's not there…"

"I know, we'll need to find another way around." I glance at the box he mentioned. It looks closed, but looks can be deceiving.

Carl gets off his quad and walks to the box, opens it, and holds out a key. He steps to the gate, unlocks it, and swings open the barrier. One hand waves us through.

I look back, and he's put the lock back on the gate and is stuffing the key into his pocket.

"Don't want the township to fine them for leaving the gate open." He winks. "Anyway, it'll keep them from following us. I left the lock on it, but it's not clasped. I say we clasp it on the way back."

"Good thinking." I feel a little more confidence with what's happening now. Carl seems to have at least a little bit of a brain when it comes to this stuff. "The light's almost gone, we need to hurry."

He jumps back on his quad, makes a motion, and guns the machine.

We head into the quarry at sixty, trying to keep the trailers from spilling as we rush over the gravel road. The first weigh station passes by quick and the devastation the quarry is having on the land spills out before us. There are fifteen pits in my area alone. Why we have so many in only twenty square kilometres is beyond me, but they are there. Probably corruption in the town's office, just like Carl said.

A corridor of trees line the dirt road and then we pop out into an open pit area. This one is longer, but not as wide. Carl heads for a mass of green reaching into the sky to the north and I follow. The ground is broken and abused in this pit, so we slow down to just over forty. My trailer bounces on the back of the bike and I hope with a little weight it'll settle down for the return trip.

Carl heads more to the north as a dark area spreads before us. The smell of sewage hits me. This must be where the septic pumpers dump when they get full. I hold my breath, hoping we can pass by them without incident. And by that, I mean without me puking.

We slow right down to get through a small line of trees and find ourselves on a packed path. Both of us open up the bikes as the path straightens out.

A sharp turn, slow turn, and then a wide open field greets us. We're on the gun club property.

The clubhouse is on our left as we make our way to the secondary building. We stop beside it, sheltered from anyone who comes down the access road.

Carl removes his helmet, the rest of us follow his example.

"Nice ride." Carl puts his helmet on the front of the quad and dismounts. "I'll definitely have to come and do this when there's no trailer behind me." He helps Jill dismount. Seems like there's hope for him yet.

I put my helmet on the side mirror and step down. My ass is sore, but nothing compared to how my shoulder is screaming at me. At least the pain is more a throb instead of the white hot poker from when I got shot. "We could make a day of it. Gas up the bikes, bring the women, run around the pit."

He stares at me for a second.

"Yeah, I like that. Pack a lunch or something. That is, if Mindy feels up to it."

I'm starting to like the guy, even if he gets on my nerves a little. Jill is smiling. She probably thinks I'm doing this for her, but really, I'm doing for all of us. If we get along, then we can survive.

"Well, you know where we're going, so lead on, McDuff." He extends his arm toward the building giving a slight bow.

I grab my bow and quiver from the back of the quad and nock an arrow. Jill does the same. Carl pulls out a gun with a long barrel, then I notice a suppressor on the end of it. Illegal in Canada, but great for what we need. Carl winks when he sees my expression.

The kid, Billy, pulls a knife from his belt. I wonder how good that would be against an attacking horde of corpses then figure it's just as good a weapon as any. He hustles his skinny ass up the three steps and reaches for the door handle.

"Wait," I say, loud enough for him to hear but not yelling. "We don't know what's in there."

"Guns, just like you said."

"Yeah, but what else?" I come up the steps, stand beside him. "Unless you like fending off a bunch of corpses, take the time to understand what's happening in the building you're going to enter." I press my ear up against the door, frown. There's a scent of decay hanging around the place but I can't figure out where it comes from. I tap lightly on the door. The sound of feet shuffling accompanied by a moan tells me I was right. "Yeah, at least one."

I reach out and motion for Carl to come up. He climbs two steps, aims his gun at the door, and nods.

The door's unlocked. It swings in easily. Five sets of milky eyes glance at us in the dying light.

"Fuck!" I raise my bow, let loose an arrow. It strikes the first corpse below the ear. I was aiming for the eye, but it works just as well. The thing goes down in a lump. Two bullets whiz past my ear as the unmistakable muffled pop of a suppressed gun goes off. Two more fall to the ground. Jill's arrow spears another in the eye and the last one lumbers toward us.

The kid steps forward before I can say or do anything. He raises his knife and first sticks the thing right in the heart. Hands with rotten flesh reach and grasp him. He pulls the knife out. A mouth opens up.

I can't see enough past the kid to get a clean shot. All I know is he's in trouble. I dive at him. My right shoulder catches the kid in the midsection and my bow falls to the ground. Three shots muffle out of Carl's gun. I look back, two arrows are sticking out of the corpses' left eye, the other side of its skull has a big hole in it from Carl's bullets.

The kid scrambles up from under me. "Fuck! Why'd you do that?"

Carl taps me on the shoulder, extends his hand. I grab it and he hauls me up. He's pretty strong for a skinny guy.

Jill steps up to the kid and slaps him. "He just saved your life." She bends and picks up the knife. Dark blood covers the blade. "Sticking one of those in the heart will only get you killed." She grabs the kid by the jaw, places the knife under his ear lobe at a 45 degree angle. "You have to kill the brain like this."

The kid's eyes are wide.

I put a hand on Jill's shoulder. "Enough, he gets the point."

"He better." Jill lowers the knife but keeps holding his jaw. "If he does a brain dead stunt like that again, we might as well kill him than save him. He puts the rest of us in danger when he does something like that."

The kid stumbles back a little, hand messaging his jaw. Red finger marks grown on the skin. "I would have killed it if you gave me a chance."

I step over to the door. "In this life, kid, you only get one chance to kill those things with a knife. Count yourself lucky we were here."

It's dark inside the building. The last of the evening light does not penetrate the iron barred windows. The stink of decay is stronger inside, especially with those corpses having been locked up. I pull out my flashlight and turn it on. Three others beams join mine and I point out the monitors sitting atop a desk in the corner.

"The feed from the main servers is from there. The storage for the guns is downstairs." I point to the staircase leading down. "We should be careful."

Noise of feet shuffling about comes up from downstairs along with the growl most of the corpses emit when they see someone who is alive. I estimate maybe three or four more.

Carl walks over to the stairs, lifts up his gun, and fires off a few muffled shots.

"I need to get one of those," Jill whispers to me. "The silencer is perfect."

There's an agreement between us about that. I remind myself to ask Carl for a suppressor when we're done here.

"Clear," he says, and starts to climb down the stairs.

"This is too easy," I say, but follow Carl into the inky darkness below.

The basement is neat, unless you count the corpses Carl shot, and the layout is simple. One big room with a door on a wall. The door has a combination lock on it. I approach it, shine my light, and reach out with one hand to start turning. A suppressed gunshot sounds again.

"That's the last one, unless they start crawling out of the ground." Carl steps beside me. "You got the combo, right?"

"Yeah, I got the combo." My fingers twirl the lock, hitting the number 44 exactly, then 23, 88, and finally around to 90. I tug on the handle, but nothing moves. "Shit, what did I get wrong?" I spin the wheel, start over again. Same outcome. "I'm not insane."

"What's wrong?" Carl shines his light at the door. "Why isn't it opening?"

"If I knew that do you think we'd still be on this side of the door?" I stare at him. "Sorry, they had to give me the combo in order to get in and out of the safe so I could install the cameras. I memorized it. I swear."

Carl taps the side of his head. "Did it ever occur to you that they gave you a secondary number for limited access and removed it? Or maybe they gave you the number and changed it when you left?"

I'm an idiot. Of course they did. Just as I left I joked to them about changing the combo of the safe. They would have done that out of necessity, for there's no reason for me to have access to it after I left.

"Probably right. Got any ideas?"

Carl smiles. "Just one." He stares at the steel door for a second. "Yup, just one." He turns, starts for the stairs, and calls back, "Don't do anything until I return." Soon he's gone.

After a few minutes he returns, a small tubular device in hand with a circular end. He's whistling. "Never leave home without it."

He comes up to the door, angles himself and blocks me off from seeing what is happening. There is a whine and then metal cries as sparks fly. Three minutes and he steps back. "Cracked." He reaches out with one hand and pulls the door open.

I'm shocked. Jill is laughing. The kid doesn't know what to say but "Cool." Carl hands me the small handheld circular saw. "Carbine blade." He winks. "Cuts through just about anything."

I heft the little thing, then hand it back to him. "Next time, let me know when you have any nice little toys hanging around."

"Saw it upstairs near the door. Whole bunch of handheld tools. We should grab them as well."

"Let's just get the rifles." I step into the storage area. "That way we can say job well done and come back for the other stuff later."

We haul six crates out, all full of automatic weapons. Not sure why they had them, but it's good for us. Two cases of ammo, about enough for 500 rounds each weapon. It should be enough to keep us safe. Carl and Jill want to take more, but it's best to keep our activity to a minimum lest anyone else comes around. As it is, we may run into someone while leaving. Better safe than sorry.

I decide to make this the last batch we'll get today as we climb down the stairs. There's a few crates with a cover over them. With swift shift, I uncover one crate marked M8. I go to open it and Carl grabs my arm.

"Those are quarter sticks of dynamite. I'd rather come back for them when we have more time."

"Good idea."

The gunning of an engine outside makes us stop. I give Carl a hard look. He nods and heads for the stairs. A quick gesture to Jill and Sonny make them come over. "Let's get this door secured so it looks locked."

We close the door and Sonny puts a little gum in the jam. Not enough to truly secure it, but at least it'll stay closed for our next raid in a few days.

Carl comes back down the stairs. "There's a car full of bikers heading to the clubhouse." He's pointing in the general direction. "They appear drunk."

My mind whirls.

Jill is the first to speak. "Are they going into the club house?"

"Yeah, looked like they were going to."

"Let's check."

Both Carl and her climb the steps, only to return a few minutes later.

"Yeah, they went into the club house." She turns to Billy. "How fast can you run?"

The kid just looks at her blankly for a second. "Pretty fast, why?"

"I have a plan, but you need to be able to run for it to work."

Billy looks at Jill, then me, finally resting his gaze on Carl. "I can run pretty fast. Faster than most of the kids in school."

Jill smiles. "Well, we have something there. Can you hotwire a car if you need to?"

"I've never gone to jail."

"No, I didn't ask if you went to jail, just if you know how to hotwire a car."

"Don't think so, but who says I have to hotwire a car?"

"Well, we need a distraction in order to get the guns out of here safe. I want you to steal their car and drive it close to the road. Not fast, or they may stop chasing you. Just enough that they start to catch up, then fall a little behind, then catch up again. Think you could do that?"

Billy nods.

Jill stares into his eyes. "Once you're near Concession 4, drive the car at a tree, but make sure you're out of it before it hits. Run to the pit and meet us where we went into the trees. Got it?"

Billy smiles. I've seen that type of smile on kids before, the one that says the grownups are letting them get dirty by playing in the mud.

Chasing Tail

I sit in the bushes with one of the assault rifles at the ready, a clip inserted, and two in my jacket pocket. Billy said to not worry, but of course I disagreed with him. That's the difference between youth and age, one believes they're invincible and the other knows better.

The kid walks out of the building, glances about, and walks over to the car.

He takes his time, runs a hand across the side, looks in the window, and points for me to see what's happening.

Billy jumps into the biker's car and starts it. The engine revs up and he screams out the window. Then the wheels of the car spin, digging into the ground, and throw dirt behind it. The car speeds down the road a couple of metres and skids to a stop.

The mop top head of Billy sticks out the window. "This is fuckin' the bomb! Hey you hairy bikers, did you know this shit is real!"

One of the bikers, a tall bald headed one, steps out of the club house, gun leveled.

Billy ducks back inside the car and hits the gas. The biker squeezes off two shots, one hitting the rear window.

The three other bikers rush out of the club house. One pulls at the big guy's arm.

"Fuck, Bull, that's our ride!"

The car stops, red tail lights blazing.

"I must of got 'em!" Bull yells.

All four rush off the porch toward the car. They get within ten metres and the lights go off and dirt spits out from the tires while the car speeds away.

The bikers run after it and out of sight.

"That was too easy," I say, getting up from my crouched position.

Jill and Carl are already at the quads, both have engines purring, loaded, and ready to go. I climb on mine and slip on the helmet.

"Let's get the kid," Carl says, and heads down the path.

I follow, and with the faceplate down I don't have to worry about eating dirt.

As soon as we hit the cover of the trees, we both turn on our lights. The moon is not full, so it doesn't throw enough light to see at the worst of times. We break out of the other side by the pits.

In a few minutes, Billy comes out of the trees about 30 metres away. His outline against the dark sky runs toward us and we wait. A gunshot echoes through the pit. Billy's body jerks and he falls forward. I no longer see him in the shadows.

"Fuck!" Carl says. "I think they got him."

"I have to know."

"No!" screams Jill. "He's fallen, and you can't see shit in this light. We need to go. Now."

A battle wages in my mind about this command. The kid is down and needs to be rescued. But she's right. How the hell am I going to find him in the dark?

To make my mind up, Bull erupts from the forest, gun at the ready. He's about 40 metres away and fires at us.

I hit the gas, turn the quad, and rush after Carl and Jill as they show the way out of the pit.

We pull into my back lot, turn off the quads, and throw tarps over them. Once the machines are hidden, I stomp to the house, tossing my helmet aside.

Mindy stands at the door, holding it open for us to come inside. She watches and I see the question in her eyes as the three of us take off our coats.

"Where's Billy?"

"He didn't make it," Jill says, wiping a tear from her eye.

"What?"

Carl slumps down on a chair. "He sacrificed himself for us. For all of us."

Mindy leans against the wall. "We lost someone." She puts a hand on her stomach, eyes wide, and runs to the bathroom. The sound of her vomiting reaches the kitchen.

"That sounds bad," Carl says.

"Yeah, she's being a trooper about it though." I stand up. "Want a rum?"

"Sure, a double." Carl glances at Jill. "You made that batch of beer yet?"

"Six bottles in the basement."

"Should I get one for you?" Carl stands.

"No, they're not ready yet." Jill glances at me. "Can I get one also?"

"Sure." I pour three rums, bring them over, and hand a glass to each. "To Billy."

We clink glasses and take a stiff drink. I feel like shit. No energy, my stomach rolling, shoulder aching. Shit, Billy deserved better.

"There was nothing we could have done," Jill says, finishing her drink. "He wanted so badly to come with us, to prove his worth."

I put my glass down. "Does he have any family?"

"Not alive," Carl says. "His mother died last month. She was going through treatment for cancer when the shit hit. No chemo."

"Fucking sucks." Jill puts her glass down. "Surviving cancer only to have the world fuck up and take you from a kid."

Mindy comes into the kitchen, blushing a little. "Sorry about that."

Carl stands up, motions Mindy to sit down. I'm really starting to like him.

"Thanks," Mindy says.

"We have weapons, now what?" Carl takes another sip.

"I don't think they'll be running their bikes for a while, so maybe we'll be on close to even ground." I grab the rum bottle, pour another shot for myself, and hold it out to Carl. He waves it away.

We sit, each engrossed in our own thoughts until Samantha comes into the room carrying a mouse in her mouth.

Carl and I wear white snow suits as we speed through the forest on our sleds. The early February air freezes my skin but I push it back, hoping we can put up with the cold.

We follow the railway tracks up past Wagg and Concession 4, sprinting over the roads as fast as possible.

For some reason, Carl is a good backyard mechanic. He tricked out the sleds with hyper muffler systems, making us almost silent as long as we didn't push them too hard.

We took helmet radios from a shop in Stouffville three days ago. Nothing fancy, just a few kilometres range. We keep in contact with each other, and I can hear his thoughts on why we take the route we're on. He wants to come up at the top of the town on the west side, hitting the hospital before the bikers know what's going on. We could be in and out in very little time was his argument.

My radio clicks on. "It's nice being active again, instead of waiting for them to take another one of us down." Carl's mike clicks off.

We're still about fifteen minutes away from our destination, but using the road would be a dead giveaway to the bikers. They've been patrolling the roads more often since our raid on the gun club.

Carl and I picked up the last of the guns a few weeks ago, making sure the booze in the club house all got a good lacing of rat poison. We found a few bodies a week later, all with the back of their heads blown out. I'm sure they were shot after dying from the poison, for they didn't have that corpse look.

O'Beirn Road flies by, then Owen, and finally Concession 6. We slow down so our passage is as silent as possible.

There are a few corpses in the snow now. They stare with blank eyes from where they lay frozen, partially covered. They're all statues stuck in place, now that the cold has set in.

I key my mike as we hit a curve in the track. "Our goal should be on the right soon."

Carl slows, then goes off the tracks into a field. I follow, seeing the copter sitting on the pad, covered in snow. Such a waste of money. I key my mike again. "You think that chopper has anything in it we could use?"

"Probably a defib and bandages. Other than that, I think they take bags onboard with them."

"You know how to fly one?" I could just see the faces of the bikers if we took off in it.

"You kidding? I'm a trucker, not a pilot."

We pull up to the back of the emergency area. Our helmets come off and I put on my ski mask, covering my face. This decision came from Cindy. She mentioned that some of the people were getting harassed by the bikers, taking pictures of them for future reference. This way, if we are seen, they'd have no way of identifying us.

Carl carries an M4 with his rucksack while I have a shotgun and bow with mine. I nock an arrow, nod to Carl, and do a crouching run to the corner of the building. If someone saw us come in, they'd be out there now. So I take only a second to get my bearings and head to the entrance.

The doors slide open with a little push and there is enough light coming in to make it easy to move about. Carl rushes in and opens the next doors as I let go of the first pair. I run through and he follows, letting go of his doors.

We pass bodies rotting on the ground. They have either bullet holes or part of their skulls blown off. It looks like a madman ran through shooting anyone they saw. I point to the crash cart against the wall, but Carl waves it away.

"More stuff a little further in."

He quick-walks a few steps, then stops in front of a door marked as the dispensary. I now know what he meant. The door lets in no light, even with the small split between the bottom and top.

Carl tries the door, but it doesn't move.

"You got the bar?" I motion to his rucksack.

He leans the M4 against the wall and unslings the bulky pack. A flashlight turns on and he tosses it up to me. "It doesn't stink in here."

I sniff a little. "It does. Maybe you're stuffed up."

"Don't think so." He hefts a crowbar and pushes it into the jam. "I can smell that fart you let go when running past me." He grunts while putting a little weight into breaking the jam.

"Maybe you smell your own diaper."

Part of the jam breaks away. "Yeah, maybe. It filled up watching you drive your sled."

I grab the bar from him, stick the end between the dutch doors, and heave. A snap rings out and the bottom is free.

"After I loosened if for you." Carl takes back the bar, shoving it into the sack.

"Yeah, you jammed it together really good." I take the flashlight and shine it into the room. "Looks like we need a few more bags."

"I'm surprised the bikers didn't find this place." Carl slides into the room.

"Probably concentrating on the drug stores." I slide into the room. "Easier to take from there with everything laid out like it is." I flash the light around, finding exactly what I need. "You got Doc's list?"

"Yeah," Carl says. "I don't know how good some of it is. This one expired last month."

"Take it anyway, depending on what it is, the expiry date may be just a crapshoot the government wanted to force on us." I scoop a couple of boxes of syringes into my bag.

We work, not bothering with anything until our bags are full. Carl finishes well before me and helps with the list I have which includes many things used to help with pregnancies, at least to Doc.

Once my bag is full, I release a breath.

Carl slides his bag under the door. "You ready to go?"

"Sure am." I slide mine after his.

We exit the room, grab our sacks, and head to the doors.

An engine backfires outside, making Carl and I skid to a stop.

"Fuck!" I glance at Carl. "We need to get out of here, right now."

"This way." Carl heads deeper into the hospital, back the way we came. He goes past the dispensary, and turns left onto a staircase. Without pause, he goes up, taking two steps at a time.

My knees scream as I follow him. Hell, I hate climbing stairs. We hit a landing and turn to the last set of steps to the second floor. Carl pushes into a small area with round tables and chairs. I see a rail for trays. Must be the café.

Carl heads right to the outside patio, pushing open the door. "Outside. We can drop to the ground from here. It's only just over three metres."

I glance over. "Little more than four if you ask me."

He tosses his bag to the ground. "Then hang."

I throw my sack over and slip over the edge. My fingers cry at the cold metal, and I let myself drop to the ground. It comes up quick, and pain erupts. I bite down on my lip, grab at my foot, and roll onto my back.

Carl lands beside me. "What happened?"

"Landed like an idiot."

He looks at my foot. "Nothing I can do here. We need to get back."

"Tell me something I don't know."

"Can you stand?"

"Not without help."

He puts my arm around him and lifts. I don't think the ankle is broken, but definitely twisted.

"Think you can drive the sled?"

"I can try."

He lowers me onto the snow mobile, then climbs on his. We wait for any sound that would tell us what's going on.

"Maybe I should take a look to see what's happening," Carl says.

A hollowness fills my guts. Last time I separated someone from the group, they died. Last thing we need is for Jill to lose Carl, she's grown attached to him over the last month.

"We can wait it out," I suggest.

"No, not if they start to come around the hospital." He dismounts. "Besides, if there's only a few..." He pats the weapon in his arms.

"Don't get yourself dead. Jill will never forgive me. For some reason, she's grown really fond of you."

One corner of his mouth lifts. "Fond? Got news for you, she'll probably be moving in."

He stalks away in a crouch before I can think of a witty comeback. So much for keeping my family together.

My finger hovers over the ignition button, anticipating Carl to either scream out in pain or come back. Waiting is something I usually don't do well. Either I'm surfing YouTube or watching something while the task is being done behind the scenes. This time is no exception. After what feels like a year, Carl comes over and mounts his machine.

"Nothing. They must have driven past and the engine backfired."

I nod, put on my helmet, and hit the ignition. "Going to have to take it a little slow. My fucking ankle is killing me."

We skim along the tracks until O'Beirn, then use that road. When we hit the end, a quick run through the forest puts us on Wees Road. That takes us to Concession 2, and the farmer's fields are the shortcut into Balantrae. Soon we're at Doc's door and unpacking the supplies. Doc looks at my ankle and orders me to keep off it for a few days. He hands me some anti-inflammatories from our raid.

131

I try to hand the pills back. "Shouldn't we save these for someone in more need?"

Doc stares at me for a second. "Don't see anyone with more of a need right now." He taps the side of the bottle. "Three a day with food, unless you want gut rot. Finish off the bottle."

"I could probably get away with two a day."

"And then the pills will last past their expiration date." He turns away. "We'll need to start holistic medicine soon. A lot of stuff is going to run out and people are going to die of the stuff we cured years ago."

I hobble out with Carl helping. He has this stupid grin while lowering me onto the sled. "What's that all about?"

"You've been told by the doc." He jumps on his sled, puts on the helmet, and hits the ignition. "And if you listen to him, maybe Mindy won't kill you this time."

I think of what Mindy will say when I show up with a screwed up ankle and sigh. She'll stop me from going out on raids if this keeps happening. Not such a bad thing, it means more home time with her, and getting ready for the coming child.

Carl veers off and heads north on Concession 2. I head south, then cut into a driveway. The idea is to use the farmer's field in order to get to the back of my property. This way, only someone with a snow mobile will be able to follow, and the wind will take care of the tracks by the time they think of it and return with one.

There's a flooded pit a half klick north and I wonder if this year I'll check it out for fish. I let my mind wander a little. The fresh air is tastier than it has ever been, now that almost all the vehicles are stopped dead with no one to drive them.

Homes stand empty, or at least void of life. Some have corpses standing at windows staring out at the landscape while others have broken doors from looters. No matter what we do, there're some people who just decide to spoil a home instead of claiming it.

Our group has grown. We now have fifty people instead of the twenty-two from a few months ago. Some talk about the bikers driving them out of Uxbridge while others are from a little north. All are scared, hungry, and just about at their wits end.

Some of the group take them in. Help find an unspoiled home for them to use. Bring wood for the fire. Food to help. Only three families have left. It makes for a good feeling, helping our little community grow.

The sled jumps, jerks sideways. I spin around to take a look. As I skid sideways, I see a massive wall of corpses edging over the hill to the north.

Security

It's still mid-day, and the horde of corpses making their way across the field astonishes me. They must be only two or three hundred metres away. I glance at the ground, trying to find out what I ran over that would have damaged the snow machine so badly. There's a mangled hand sticking out of the snow. It's grasping at the air in a slow finger curling motion. I ran over a corpse buried in the snow. My stomach lurches a little as the appendage does a slow motion grasp toward me.

With nothing left to discover, I hammer the gas and turn the sled toward home. I'm only a few metres away from a line of trees. If I get there, they 'll block me from the corpses. After that, there's a hill I can go down in order to have a clear shot to the house. Generally, I like to take a roundabout way home, but this time I think it's better to get there and hunker down for the rest of the day. Besides, my ankle is screaming at me.

I count off the metres as the trees come closer. Just a little more. The back end of the sled stops. I'm thrown into the windshield. It doesn't break.

A hazy picture forms… Black dials. A buzzing. Pain in my mouth. Snow crunching. Red hits the black. A dot of blood.

I push away, head spinning, body weak and slow to respond. Everything is tilted as I float there on the sled – there's something I should be doing. I grasp the handles. A snow mobile. My thumb hits the ignition. Gears grind, then nothing. The buzzing is accompanied by a beeping. Both are receding into the distance. More snow crunches.

Something nags me in the back of my mind. I've forgotten something very important. It's not Mindy, or the child she carries. Jill? No, not my concern anymore. Carl will take care of her.

A rotting stench fills the air. I glance to the left. They're almost on me. Ten metres, maybe eleven. The advancing horde stocks at a constant pace. Bluish fingers reach out toward me. *Get away from here!*

I jump off the sled. Pain erupts in my ankle. I fall, seeing wooden spikes driven up between the front of the sled and track. Nice trick. Wait until the snow is deep enough and cover up the spikes. Someone drives over them and the back treads, which ride lower than the front on fresh snow, are wedged.

Fumbling, I push myself up on my good foot. The snow is less than a metre deep, but that's on the high side of less than a metre. It reaches just above my knees. Nothing will happen if I try to hop out of the field. Even an uninjured person would be hard pressed to struggle through this and keep ahead of the corpses. They don't tire. They don't sleep. They keep coming as long as they can either see or hear you.

My shotgun is still slung over my shoulder, so I pull it off. Not to fire, but to help stabilize myself while trying to get away.

I'm up on one foot, now the other. A hop, using the weapon as a crutch. Another foot. I head for the trees. If I can get there... Yes, if I get there ahead of the corpses maybe I can climb one and wait them out. Mindy will realize I'm late, hunt down Carl with Jill's help and come to find me – what? Frozen in a tree? Corpses eating my flesh? Dead, or even worse, alive again?

No, I have to make it to the house. If I get there, we can wait them out, shoot a few from a window, lessen their numbers while others come to help. Something we've done for the community. We all help one another. If someone is in need, we come to help them.

I hobble toward the tree line. It's slow going, but seems to be enough to keep me ahead of the horde. Hell, it even looks like I'm gaining ground. Keep it up, Steve. You have a kid on the way and a beautiful girl waiting to make another when she's able. Get home. Protect them.

Once in the trees, the ground has less snow. It makes for an easier hobble away from the advancing corpses. I'm starting to tire. There's no way I'll be able to keep this up for the time it'll take me to reach the house. I keep pushing – one ankle on fire with all the jostling and the other screaming at me from for all the work it's doing. The shotgun's probably screwed up by now, the barrel filled with snow and ice. I should have used it the other way, but then the risk would be it going off and removing my arm just under the armpit.

There's a tree up ahead, its wide expansive trunk inviting me to take cover behind it. My breath is coming in and out fast. Sweat beads on my forehead, falling, and hitting my heavy parka. It's freezing on the surface, not running anywhere past the fluffy collar of the hood. I place my hand on the tree and stop hopping for a few seconds. Allow my body to slow down. Cool off. There's a desire to strip the heavy coat, but that could be a problem. Lowering my temperature fast will only bring on sickness. Puffs of steam exit my mouth. Sweat stops running, instead it forms beads of ice on my face.

Crushing of snow. Snapping of twigs. The horde has entered the forest. They're still following me.

I push away from the tree. Lumber forward. Move faster. My heart starts to hammer more than before. I break out the other side of the small forest. The field before me is a blanket of white. Nothing but level open ground. Easy to get across. Easy for the corpses.

Nothing is left but to keep pushing myself. One foot. Hobble with the makeshift crutch. One foot. I keep the rhythm going, hear the corpses following. Don't glance back. They're either way behind you or about to reach out and grab a hold. I push even harder.

There's a goffer hole or something. It swallows part of the shotgun. I stumble, fall forward. Tuck. Roll. Then I'm staring at the sky. Little wispy clouds hover before me. But I need to keep going. Need to make it home. Make it to Safety.

I roll to my side. The corpses have made it through the forest. There's something about them now. They're not as fast. Lumbering a little slower.

No time to think about it. I raise up and push off, limping on my throbbing feet, using the injured one to bear the weight as much as it can stand. No telling what type of damage I'm doing to the muscles. Doc'll kill me for this. Heck, Mindy will kill me. And even if I don't survive, she'll hunt me down like a rabid dog.

I make it to Lapier Street. Not much farther to go. My heart is bursting inside. Throat raw. Both legs screaming at me to stop. But I go on. The numbness of cold infiltrates the front of my good leg. It brings about a more bearable pain.

The Sherpas in the Himalayans have always been able to push past the cold. I try to channel their spirit. They probably don't have the hell we have to live with today. No corpses would walk in the frozen world there. But here. Here they walk. It's not as cold, bitter, or barren as it is there.

I'm crossing Goodwood Street now. Almost in my back yard. Past my back-neighbour's house, through the pool area, I hit the fence. Maybe I'm going to make it.

A hand grasps at my coat. It pulls at me. The stench of rotting meat assaults my nose.

I'm not going to make it.

This is where death will take me. Mindy. I'll never see her again. Unless. I unzip. Let the coat go. Roll over the fence. Land in the snow. Cold encompasses me. I look up. One corpse. It bites into the coat, not realizing there is no one in it. Another comes up beside, staring at me with milky eyes. It pushes against the fence. I realize if enough of them do that, the one barrier protecting me will crumple, and then they can reach their goal.

I roll. *Get up!* Hobble toward the house. I'm going to make it.

Mindy throws another log on the fire and closes the front. The flames dance on the new fuel as the wood catches fire. She adjusts the dampener the way I taught her and more air enters the sealed unit. Warm. I'm finally getting warm.

They have me back on the foldout bed. Three heavy blankets cover my shivering body. Jill comes around from the kitchen, mug of tea in one hand, thermometer in the other.

"Where the fuck do you think that's going?" I reach out to take the mug, keeping my backside away from her.

She gives me that wicked smile. I've seen it on her face before. One corner of her mouth is higher than the other. "Want to bend over and find out?"

Samantha jumps up on the bed, walks over to me, and flops down, back resting against my side. "If I do that, Sam will have to move."

Mindy comes over and sits on the side of the bed. "Oh, don't interrupt Sam's sleep for God's sake. She's so busy napping that it would be a shame to wake her up." She reaches out and rumples the cat's fur. "Besides, if she's down here, I won't have to push her off the bed when she tries to lay on my bladder."

Jill gives the thermometer a shake. "Well, open up."

I do, and she inserts the thing into my mouth.

"Not as much fun for me than the other way, but I guess that'll do." Jill takes the cup away from me. "Nothing until I get a good reading."

They're mothering me. Jill, because she likes to boss people around, and Mindy, because she wants me to be around for a while. I put up with it because I know they actually care. After a minute, Jill hands me my tea, pulls the thermometer out, and stares at the number.

Mindy glances up. "Well?"

Jill just snorts. "He's down a little. Probably because he's no longer full of shit."

I let out a bark.

"You need to make sure he stays warm until his internal temp comes back up. If it spikes, we'll need to get Doc involved." Her smile hits both sides of her mouth. "And that way he can shove this up your ass like he does with the cat."

I cough. "That's the cat's thermometer?"

"I don't know. It said Sam on the label. Is that the one he shoves up her ass?"

"Will you two stop it?" Mindy takes my hand. "God, yes, she's going to be living with Carl." Her eyes search out Jill's. "Yes, you're welcome to come here any time you want."

"Yes," I echo. "Hell, Jill, Carl's a good guy. If ever you two need anything, just come by and ask. Our door is always open for the both of you."

Jill sneers at us. "Why would I want to come back here?"

She puts up a good front, but there's a tear welling that she quickly swipes away before turning her back on us. "Maybe I will, just to see the cat."

"Sure," I say. "I bet Sam'll miss you. She loves sleeping on your bladder."

"A few of the new people told me something interesting." She turns back, eyes under control but a little red. "It seems the bikers have been putting up a fence on the north part of Uxbridge. That's why we're seeing more corpses coming through here."

"A fence?" I wonder what it means.

"Yeah, a long chain linked one. Not too tall, about maybe a metre and a half."

Just enough to be as tall as the average person, but not so tall as to be an issue to climb. "They're doing this in the winter?"

"From what they said, the fence is being braced up for the winter, then they plan to make it permanent once spring comes by. This way they have it in place sooner than later."

"Maybe they want to wall off the town for protection." I think more about what it means. They will live better without having to wait for corpses to wander by. It means protection. Better living. Building a community. "Did they say how far across they are?"

"Someone said Concession 6, but that was a few days ago." Jill takes a deep breath. "If they're building it quick, they could have the northern part of the town secured before spring, and then they could look at enclosing the place before winter. If we want to get rid of them, we'll need to do something soon."

"That's why they haven't been out much." I sip the tea. "I don't think my little accident was just that. Someone had to plant those spikes just at the right angle to drive into the track. And putting it in such an out of the way place is weird. Why would anyone spike a field like that?"

Mindy gives Sam one last belly rub and stands. "I don't know, but what I do know is you guys will need to start taking different routes in order to get home. Someone must have been watching you for a while to know which way you'd take." She walks to the fireplace, adjusts the damper, and comes back to the edge of the bed. "The only good thing that's come out of this is you get to take two weeks off from any scouting or raiding until that ankle heals."

Mindy groans as she climbs the stairs to the second floor. I have a hard time believing that she's pregnant when looking at her from behind, but once she turns, you can tell. She's made me stay on the foldout for two weeks, and now I'm ready for my own bed.

My ankle is more an orange than a grapefruit, and a little weight on it is okay. Doc stopped by yesterday to make sure and proclaimed me on the mend. Now all I have to do is exercise the thing.

Jill moved out last week. Carl came over, apologized for not making sure I made it home, then helped her pile all her stuff into his truck. Never knew she collected as much as she had. Where did all those clothes come from?

Mindy hugged her and cried. I shook Carl's hand and handed over a bottle of rum. Need to get some more soon, down to my last three bottles. He took it with thanks and they both fled the house. Probably to romp around his place naked and have sex. I don't think they did it in our place and it took a long time before Jill let him be alone with her.

I put an arm around Mindy, kiss the top of her head. "They grow up so fast."

She lets out a little laugh. "I'll need some maternity clothes soon."

"Woman, I'm going to keep you barefoot and preggies for the next twenty years."

A slight blush colours her cheeks. "Want to practice some?"

"Best request I've had all week."

She takes my hand and leads me upstairs.

As I push the quad out of the garage, the crisp early March air tells me we're in for a warm summer again. Water drips from icicles on the roof and I wonder how much longer the solar panels will hold up. They need to be inspected, broken ones replaced, and converters changed. Normally that would be for someone fully trained in the process, but being the only person who knows anything about the technology, it falls on me to do it.

The quad needs to be up and running for the spring weather. The sled also needs to be replaced this year.

I pull the plugs, check to make sure they have life left, then put them back. The battery is connected next and I thumb the ignition. The small starter chugs and the motor catches. It idles rough for a few minutes then smooths out. Once it reaches a low rumble, I turn it off.

The small jack lifts the quad and I slide a catch bucket under it. The oil will go into a recycler, and from there it'll be turned into fuel for something. Not sure what, because I haven't filled the barrel yet, but something that runs on hybrid fuel or something.

I change out the oil filter and fill it back up with the synthetic we found. Need to refresh the fuel stabilizer stock or the gas will go bad.

Should be good to go for a year at least. Then we have to worry about how we're going to get around. Wonder how the bikers are doing it?

The engine comes to life with a touch of the ignition. I drive it through the garage and into the back. Time to do the other one.

My gaze lands on the fence as I drive to the back of my property. I see a mass of white fabric waving in the slight breeze. A close examination shows my winter parka, or what remains of it, catching the wind. I think about the hordes travelling through the fields from somewhere. We really need to find out what's going on and why so many of them congregated on their walk across the country.

I shake myself out of the dream world. Nothing to do right now. A few twists and the battery is swapped into the other quad and I start it up. The thing complains to no end as the once dormant engine finally catches. I let it rumble for a while and then throw it into gear. It dies about half way to the garage. I thumb the starter again, but the engine doesn't catch. Could be the gas.

A few twists and the cap is off the gas tank and I see it's empty. I have a habit of filling tanks and adding stable before storing, and I know this one was full at the start of winter.

Getting off the quad, I check the cut-off. It's not on, so that could explain why the gas drained. But something is bothering me.

Sharp pain erupts in the back of my head, then the whole world goes black.

Train Ride

I see the tops of trees pass by me. A clank sounds four times. Someone swears. My eyes sting. A face full of hair comes into view. Gray, long hair tumbles down over shoulders and a bird's nest of a beard hides the mouth. He scowls and bends over, taking my jaw in his hands. I try to bat away his hands but mine are non-responsive. A gun comes into view, held by the man with the hair-encrusted face. Darkness takes me as he hits me with the butt of the weapon.

Rough hands grab me by the coat and haul me off the ground. I open my eyes to a fading light, and fall forward when I'm placed on my feet. Ground kisses my face. I manage to roll a little before those rough hands grab at me again and set me up on wobbling feet. That hair-encrusted face is before me again. Pale blue eyes squint from behind bushy eyebrows. I know where I am now. The train station in the centre of Uxbridge.

"You've been giving our people a hard time," Hairy Face says. His breath reminds me of raw sewage pumped from a septic tank. "I don't know if you have any idea who you're dealing with."

The pieces start to come together. The jail cell, Sonny raped Jill before we rescued her, the bikers at Wallymart, the gun club.

Hairy Face takes out a Smith and Wesson, pulls back the hammer, and points it at my chest. "Those supplies, the ones from the hospital, those were ours." He puts his hand on my shoulder. "And before that, your people have been emptying all the stores in the outskirts of our town for the last few months."

My head bobs down. He grabs my hair and pulls up my head. "Stay with me, now." His voice is soft, gentle, nothing like the hate-filled eyes behind the bushy eyebrows. "You need to know what's going to happen to you."

He lets my head go and I manage to keep it from falling. Pain lances behind my eyes from the two hits and I wonder if I have a concussion. Best if I do. If my brain swells up, I'll be dead-dead. Not a walking corpse dead, but truly the not coming back to eat anyone dead. Mindy will be okay, so will the child. Carl and Jill will make sure of that.

"Bull, give me a cigar."

He holds out a hand as the tall bald guy puts a stubby into his hand. "Thanks."

"No problem, Pa."

I wince at the name. It's not something the bikers do up here. Only the big US types call each other family. They use titles like Pa, Ma, Son, Uncle. Each designates who they are in the organization. Being Pa means you've proven yourself as a badass, able to do just about anything to make sure the rules of the gang are followed. Sort of like the police of the group, but with nothing to stop them from caving someone's head in to get the point across.

He sticks the cigar in his mouth, pulls a gold zippo out of his pocket, and lights it. "Something you gotta know about me." He puffs a little, making the cigar end glow. "I'll do anything to make sure people understand the message. And you, well, you don't understand very much, do you?"

"I have a kid." It comes out without prompting.

"I had a kid, once. Nice kid. Wife was pregnant with our second. My little girl lived for about three hours while the medics tried to save her mother. She was struck from behind by another car." He takes a pull off the cigar, blows smoke out. "Drunk driver took their lives away from me. He walked away without a scratch. Slap on the wrists was all the court gave 'im." He takes another pull. "Ya see, he was rich. Lots of money. Not like some of the punks who say they're rich and need to borrow money, I'm talking Walmart rich. Ate caviar every morning on little stale toast and had someone wipe his ass after taking a shit."

His eyes stare over my shoulder while he speaks.

"They didn't even let me attend my wife and child's funeral. Too

143

DOUGLAS OWEN

much of a risk." He uncocks the gun, places it in a holster. "So I kept my nose clean until parole came up. A shining example of a model prisoner. Even studied a little medical stuff so it looked like I could contribute to society."

I'm light headed, unable to focus. He reaches out, puts a hand on my cheek.

"You still with me?"

"Please, let me go back to my wife. My child."

He lets out a little laugh. "But I haven't finished my story yet." He drops the hand, takes a long pull off the cigar. The end blazes like the fires of hell, but it's gentler than the man's eyes. "When I got out of prison, the first thing that happened is my family here handed over the keys to my hog and an address. The saddle bags were full of everything I would need. So, I drove to the address. Do you know whose address it was?"

"I don't," I manage to get out.

"Well, it was the guy who killed my wife and child. My family wanted to make sure I had nothing to keep me from being part of their lives. You see, wanting revenge is the worst thing a person can deal with in life." He places his hand on my shoulder again. "So they told me to take my time. I did."

He reaches into his pocket, pulls out some photographs. "Here's my wife. Beautiful, isn't she?" He puts a picture down of a woman in her mid-thirties, tattoos covering her arms and throat. A leather jacket hangs on her shoulders. She's smiling, and I notice one tooth is missing.

"And this is my daughter." He puts another picture down. A girl, maybe five, sits at a table drawing with crayons. She has shoulder length blonde hair and pale blue eyes. The kid looks nice, cute, but what can you tell from a photograph.

"I miss them every day. But I don't need to be with them, not yet. And that is why they trust me. I've shown that I don't need to be with my wife and child because I'm alive. Not like those things walking around today. Or like the people who'd take supplies from a hospital when people are relying on them. So where did you take the supplies?" He puts a hand under my chin, makes me look right at him.

"If you let me go, I'll take you to them."

He shakes his head. "No, I don't think that would be a good idea." He lets my head go. "You see, when I rolled up to the guy's place after

144

getting out of prison, I asked myself if I could ever let him live. The answer was no. But if he could bring my wife and kid back to life, I'd let him die fast."

Bull snickers a little and Pa gives him a look. The big man glances at the ground and mumbles an apology.

"When I got to his house, I couldn't believe what I saw. A huge mansion of a home. I kicked in the door and the front was done in marble with quartz inlay. You know, the type miners try to find in order to get gold. Even had some flecks of it." He takes another pull of the cigar. "The staff was nice enough. They all came running in, making it easy to kill them. Each one." He makes a gun out of his free hand and does a shooting motion. "Once they were done, I went up into the bedroom. You see, it was early in the morning when I went to him. Didn't want the guy to be somewhere else.

"Found 'im in the bathroom, cowering beside a toilet that cost more than my hog. He had a bathrobe on and nothing else. Made it easy for me to take care of the needed things. Took him downstairs and onto his patio." He looks at the cigar end, blows on it. "Used three cigars to burn the names of my wife and kids into his skin. Jullie and Hellen. Wanted them to be deep. He screamed all the while, pleading to know what I wanted. He could buy anything, he said. Had more money than God. I asked for my wife and child back."

He ground out the cigar in the dirt. "The guy went pale when I told him that. Shit right on the spot. Good thing I had him on the patio, it would have ruined one of his rugs."

His voice never changes. Flat, unwavering, like he's just reading the newspaper. "I used elastic bands to staunch the bleeding when I cut off his pecker. Put it right into his mouth when he passed out. Made for an interesting show when he woke up. Balls came off next. One at a time. You know, a person doesn't bleed to death when those things are taken from the body. For some reason, if you just stop the blood flow it'll seal itself off.

"That was the first day. And after that, I got creative in ways to deal with him."

"Please, I'll do anything."

"Did I say you could talk?" He looks sideways at me. "If I'm not mistaken, I'm telling you my story so you can know who I am. This is important if you want your little Asian girl friend to live past

145

tomorrow."

I feel sick. Not just the vomit type of sick, though that is rolling around inside, but light-headed and not able to keep going sick. The curl up and die kind of sick you get from drinking a forty of tequila.

"That night I made sure he had lots to drink. Wanted to make sure his body replenished the blood he lost. Then I put elastics around each toe. Tight enough that they went purple. Have you ever had anything turn purple when it was tied off? Lack of blood flow. Soon, the part dies unless you get blood into it soon. I left him on the patio, tied up like that. Made it so his head pointed right at his feet so he could watch how they changed colour."

He reached into his back pocket again, pulled out another photo and put it on the ground. "I tied off piece by piece of him. Cut it off before it could kill him. Let him feel the pain. He pleaded better then you."

There's no rhyme or reason to his soliloquy. He just tells me what he did to someone, maybe to make sure I understand what he's capable of, or willing to do. All I can think of is what he may do to me in order to get what he wants. What his people want. Or worse yet, what he may do to Mindy and my unborn child.

"I made sure he had enough time to really understand what he did. After five days, I put two silver dollars over his eyes so he could make his way to hell."

He tosses down the picture. My stomach roils from the sight of a man, no longer with arms, legs, nose, or teeth. His body is cut all over, lines of scabs cover what's left of him. One eye is still attached to tissue and hangs by his temple. Even the lips are cut away.

"He did beg for forgiveness in the end. Wanted to live, even with his arms and legs cut off, eyes pulled out, teeth removed. Strange on how a person thinks there's nothing worse than death. That's why you see he's not tied up in that photo."

I can't take my eyes off the horror he's put in front of me. It haunts me, tells me something like this could be my end. His speech now makes sense. He wants me to realize there's no hope for me. This is the end. I am about to die and nothing I can do will stop it. He wants the information, but wants to make sure it is real.

"You need something to drink?"

He reaches behind me and snaps a finger. Someone yanks my hair. Water is spilled into my mouth. I cough, sputter the liquid. My hair is let go and I fall forward, kissing the ground once again. Eyes fall on the picture. It burns into my mind. The thought of little pieces being cut off, one at a time, seeing my body hacked away by a madman flips a switch in me.

"There's something you need to know," he says. "I never leave home without them."

A handful of elastics land on top of the picture.

I don't know when I stop screaming. My throat is raw, eyes sore from staring at that picture. Every part of me wants to disappear into some unknown place. But nothing happens.

Two pairs of strong arms haul me to my feet. They pull at me until we reach a van. Someone opens the door while another pushes me into it. The door closes and a driver slams the thing into drive.

There are three other people in the van besides the driver. Two are unconscious while the third just cowers in the corner. He's mumbling to himself about telling everything. I'm not sure who he is, but I recognize the face from somewhere.

The truck jostles as if we're driving on a track, then smooth road. The ride is slow, the driver taking his time to get to where we're supposed to be.

"Who are you?" I ask.

"You better be quiet back there." The driver glances back. "Last thing you want is me knocking you out before we get to where we're going." He laughs.

I count the seconds. They turn into minutes. Ten go by before we turn onto a gravel road.

Something thuds against the van – light taps like someone is hitting it. Then we're climbing a steep road. Finally, after levelling out, we stop.

The driver pulls out a revolver and opens his door. He fires a few shots and I hear feet skitter away. The door closes.

Both back doors open on the van. The driver is there standing with a smile on his face. He grabs one of the limp forms and moves the body to the doors, then pulls it to the ground. Next he reaches for the other one, putting it right beside. The conscious captive I'm with starts to edge away from the doors, mumbling something about telling everything if only they'd let him go. The driver climbs in, cuffs the man, and pulls him outside as well. He then looks at me.

"You seem to be someone who has a little more brains then the rest." He leans against the van door, pulls out a pack of cigarettes, takes one, and lights it. Before putting the pack into his pocket, he stops and he looks at me, then offers a smoke. I shake my head, sending fingers of lightning pain through it.

"Suit yourself." He puts the pack away. "Pa's a little upset with you and yours. Says that all our stuff, everything that goes missing, is all your fault. We have to find you, every one of you, and make an example." He takes a deep drag, blows smoke into the air. "Me, I think some of the buggers we take in are stealing more than they need. But who am I, just a lonely Uncle."

He stands there, not a care in the world, smoking the cigarette as if he can just go buy another pack once they're done. A conundrum if I've ever seen one. But that doesn't stop him. He just keeps smoking, and the longer he takes, the more likely I can figure out how to get out of here.

"Ya see we've taken in a lot of riffraff over the last couple of months. Some from up north, others from the east, and a few from the west. What we never seem to get is those from the south. No one ever comes from the south to up here." He takes another drag. "We haven't figured it out yet. But you, you're a smart guy. I bet you've figured it out, haven't you."

I don't know if he wants me to say anything or just nod. He seems to be like Pa, so I just nod.

"See. I told them you'd know." He drops the cigarette and grinds it out with a foot. "I bet you'd tell me. Com' on, tell me why. I really want to know."

I look at the floor of the van. There's blood on it. Dried and hard. Probably at least a few months old. Who did this? Did he? Or was it someone else? Pa maybe? Either way, I don't think I'm getting out of this one alive, so I shake my head.

"And I thought you were smart." He reaches back and pulls out a bowie knife. "I should take your hands off for that, but Pa would be upset. He wants you out here for a while, get all tendered up. Then maybe he'll let me take your hands."

"Migration," I stumble out.

"What? What was that?"

148

"The reason. Migration."

He sheaths the knife, sits back on his haunches, and pulls out the cigarette pack. Out one comes and he lights it. "I don't know what you mean by migration."

I stare at him, wondering if he passed a certain grade level or just thinks he's smart. Even without an education, people should know what that means.

"During the winter, most birds migrate south to keep warm."

"Yes, I know what the word means, just not what you mean by saying it."

I glance up, stare him right into the eye. "They're migrating south for the winter. They freeze solid during the cold months so it makes sense why they're doing it." My head is splitting, but I need to keep his attention on me. Need to find a way out of the mess. "They go south in order to feed, just like the birds. Soon, they'll start heading north again because the weather is warmer. If they stay too far south they'll rot faster. Call it an ingrained instinct to survive or something. They'll move with the weather to a place that's warm but not sweltering."

"How many do you think will come north?"

"All of them."

King of the Hill

The driver stares into my eyes. At first, it looks like he's not getting the impact, then the light goes on. His eyes widen, cigarette drops, fingers twitch. I had a similar reaction when I figured it out. That's why all those walkers went north during the summer and south during the winter. The extreme hot and cold – they can't survive in it. One cooks them, makes their bodies rot quicker, the other freezes them in place, keeps them from surviving. That's what it's about, survival.

"I'll be fucked," the driver says, his voice flat.

I remember telling Mindy about it; the look of shock was similar to this man's.

He bends over, picks up the cigarette, and takes another drag. "So, you mean to say all the corpses are going to head north once the weather starts to warm up?"

"Not all of them, only the ones in the Northern Hemisphere."

"And what leads you to believe that?"

He's generally interested. Something you don't see with a criminal. Usually it's all about them. This guy is thinking of the big picture.

"During the winter, all the corpses came out of the north. During the summer when this crap all started, most of the corpses either travelled north or stayed still. The heat rots their bodies fast. Like chicken left in the sun. Once all the muscle tissue is rotted off, the corpse can't move, and finally dies. It takes a while, but it started happening to the first ones.

"In the winter, all the corpses travelled south. Maybe not in a direct line, but they went south. I found a couple of them all but frozen. They still moved, fingers clenching, jaws biting, eyes swiveling. But they couldn't move about. Stuck. So the basic is to go where they can hunt, get food, feed. The basics of survival. Like the migration of birds or herds of animals that don't hibernate."

He flicks the cigarette, letting ash drop to the van floor. "How long you recon we got?"

"Another month before they start to get up here."

His gaze moves from me to the van floor, fixing on something I cannot see. Then he looks up at me. "Have you seen our fence?"

"Yes."

"You know it curves around the top of the town, right?"

"Yes."

His finger finds the ash, pushes it until it crumbles. "What do you think of it?"

"Looks like a good fish net."

A quick harrumph comes out of him. He seems to find the statement amusing.

"Years ago I used to poach in the Montreal River near New Liskeard. Probably closer to Elk Lake. I lived on the Indian reserve there with my wife and kids." His eyes are unfocused. "I remember putting up a net while the pickerel spawned. Man, I miss eating pickerel. We usually caught fifty or sixty fish in a week. Spill out the eggs of the females and the sperm of the males, dump that and the guts back into the river. Let the fry survive. Old Injun trick. More will live off their parents' guts and the next year you get a mess more."

His gaze comes back to me. "Figure we'll survive this?"

"It depends on how they come up." I take a deep breath. There's other people around us, I can hear them. Noticed the hand of a person on the back door. The driver is sitting there on his haunches, his back to it as he's talking to me. "I figure, if they're like the birds, once they hit Hamilton, they'll spread out. Most will bypass us, take out Brampton, maybe Newmarket.

"Some could come through the lake, but I doubt that would be good for them. Fish will peck at meat that floats by and the water will accelerate the rotting process, bloat them up. Some of the fatter corpses will float, probably not get very far that way. But you never know."

I catch the glimpse of a face peeking around the door. Wild eyes, frazzled out hair, skin dark and dirty. It slips back behind the door quick

151

and I notice the driver smiling at me.

"You saw one. Good, that means they're getting brave again." He pulls out his gun. "They only scare for a little when they know you're not trying to shoot them directly." He jumps out, goes to the side of the van and out of my sight. I can hear him yelling, "Little fucks! No food today!" Bang! The gun goes off. "Starve for another day!" Bang! "Eat the unconscious ones if you're hungry!" Bang! Then silence. I count ten before he comes around and jumps back into the van. He resumes his stance.

"I have to leave you here for a few days." His voice sounds more like an apology than anything else. "Pa's orders."

He crab walks past me. "Bet your head hurts from all the times he belted you." He opens up the glove compartment, fishes around for something, then closes it.

"Best I can do." There's a small plastic bottle in his hand. He opens it, fishes out a transparent yellow capsule. "Open."

I open my mouth a little. He places the pill on my tongue, reaches to the front seat and brings over a cup. "A little water to help you swallow that. It's extra strength so it'll work fast."

He places the cup against my mouth and tips it. Cold water washes the pill down my throat. It hits my empty stomach and a rumbling echoes in the van.

"Guess you're hungry too." He leans to the front seat again, comes back with something that resembles dried meat. "Don't really care for this stuff. The guy who made it used a lot of brown sugar to help dry it out. Little too sweet for my liking."

He pulls some of it off and holds it out for me. I lean forward and take it into my mouth.

"I like talking to you. Over there I have to be dumber than the guy higher ranked than me. And some of them are real idiots. Nice to talk to someone who has a brain in their head for once." He looks out the front window. "They're getting brave again." His gaze turns back to me. "Little word of advice, kill the first one who tries to touch you. If you let them get away with anything when they see you, they'll only take all your clothes if you're lucky. If not, they'll kill and eat you." He slides back to the rear doors. "The corpses can't walk up anything more than a twenty degree angle, so you're safe as long as you don't go to the bottom of the ramp."

He motions with a hand for me to come to the doors. I think about not doing it, staying in the van where it's safe. But then I remember the other guy he pulled out, and inch to the doors.

"Turn around and I'll cut you free."

I spin around. My hands jerk a little, then they can move. I bring them around. The plastic zip ties are still there, just cut from each other. I need to get them off soon before they stop my circulation.

The driver steps back. "Come on out."

I climb out of the van, head spinning a little. The mid-day sun beats down on this late March. The temperature is above freezing and the air is crisp. I glance about and we're in one of the many pits that decorate the landscape around Uxbridge.

The driver motions me away from the van and I take a few steps forward. There's a ramp leading down and I realize we're on a raised platform in the middle of the pit. A large hut is in the middle and a steep ramp of dirt is where we came up onto this little island. Down below are corpses. More corpses than I have ever seen in one place. It's like a city's worth of dead down there, walking about. The driver smiles.

"We needed someplace to put them all. We killed a lot of them, but that wasted bullets. We used a scoop and dump trucks to herd them all together and brought them here for safe keeping. This way, we're safe from them, and they act as good guards. Never sleeping, never complaining. No strikes. Can't be bribed no matter how pretty you are." He laughs. "Not saying anyone would look at you, but they'd rather bite it than suck it." He lets out another laugh. "Oh, I'll have to remember that one. Maybe get someone to try it back home."

He stares at me for a few seconds, then reaches behind and pulls out the bowie knife. "I think you're going to need this." He extends it toward me, handle first. "Like I said, I like you. May even visit to see if you have any more ideas about these things later on. I have to bring food every couple of days. These animals"–he motions toward the hut–"they eat just about everything in sight when it's dumped for them. You seem to be someone who knows when to eat and when to store."

I take the knife, stare at the blood stained edge.

"Don't worry, mostly used to kill corpses."

He closes the doors to the van, turns, and looks at me again. "Try to survive. We don't have that many smart people left in the world. For some reason, most of the smart people died quick."

153

DOUGLAS OWEN

"Most of us didn't believe what was happening."

He stares at me for a second, head tilted a little back and to the side. There's a smile, not much of one, but still a smile. "I do like you." He turns, checks the doors. "I'll be back in a day¬ or—"

I step forward. He shifts back to face me. I slide the knife into his gut.

His eyes widen, mouth hanging open, eyebrows arching. A gurgling sound escapes his lips. He pulls down arched brows, clenches teeth, and lips curl away from his teeth. He slits his eyes at me, right hand reaching down. I pull up on the knife, slicing through muscle. A stench fills the air as intestines part. Wetness spreads onto my hand.

"I– liked– you…" The last breath leaves his body and it slumps into my arms.

The eyes stare at the sky and soon there's the sound of footsteps coming toward me cautiously. I pull back the knife and let the body slip from my arm. There's no special slugging sound like the movies, just a lifeless heap at my feet. I reach down, unsling his gun, and check the clip. A couple of rounds left. A quick search finds two more full clips, more of the jerky, and the keys. I stand and go 'round the driver's side, then stop. Children.

It all makes sense now. The town's children, the ones they would have to take care of, all left here. Why spend the manpower to watch them when the dead could do it. There are a dozen of them of various heights. Three girls, nine boys. All are dirty, with rags for clothes. They're walking toward the van in an almost sideways motion. All stop when I come around.

One of the girls, I would guess around seven, comes forward. Her little body emaciated.

I remember old black and white pictures of POWs being released by Japan after the Second World War. How their stomachs were caved in and all the muscle stripped off them. The girl looks like that. Even the hollow eyes look up at me with little hope or joy in them. Her teeth, almost black, stand behind pale lips. I slide the knife into the belt sheath.

"I'm not going to hurt you." I take a deep breath. "In fact, we're all getting out of here."

I look around for the three who came with me, but find nothing.

"We trew dem over," the tallest of the boys says. "We should trow ya over."

He starts to walk toward me. I've seen shows where tigers are not as threatening. He's still underweight, but if all of them charge and pile on me at once, then I'm done for. I start to back up, trying to keep the same distance between us.

"I can get us out of here. We can all get into the van and escape." I pass the back of the van.

"They all say that, then try to touch us where we don't want to be touched." The tall kid keeps coming forward.

"Over da edge," one of the smaller boys says. "Watch the games get played."

I wonder what he means by that, then realize it's the game of survival. To see if the corpses can tear me apart, or how long it'll take them. I keep backing up, and now they're at the back of the van.

The little girl sees the driver. She smiles, then giggles, and finally laughs. "He's got part of his insides out."

All of them stop. The big one looks over, his brows draw together. He almost starts to talk, but doesn't, mouth left open just enough.

Finally, he looks at me. "Ya sticked 'em?"

I pull out the knife. "With this."

He looks back at the body along with the others. Then they move as one toward it. I envision them sticking their hands in it, taking out the intestines and dancing around, but they don't. In fact, they lift the body up, careful not to spill any of the insides, and take it to the edge of the plateau. In one quick well organized movement, they toss the body over and start to cheer. It only lasts a second as they shuffle back.

"They don't like eating dead things," the larger one says.

"Dead. Yeah," one of the girls says.

The larger boy looks at me. "You say we going?"

I nod. "Let's get into the van."

They pile into the open back of the van. All except the larger one. He climbs into the passage seat and puts on his seatbelt. Once strapped in, he just sits there, hands on lap, staring in front. There's something about him, and I guess his age to be around fourteen, maybe sixteen at most. A little peach fuzz adorns his upper lip, but not much more. His chin sticks out, a more roman nose sits on his face, and the brows remind me of a Neanderthal. But who am I to judge. They're all alive in this hell world.

155

I shove the key into the ignition and start it up. The engine comes to life and I drop it into gear. We lurch forward, and I swing the wheel to the left, aiming for the ramp.

He didn't lie, the driver that is, the ramp is steep. I spend more time on the brakes than anything else. As we hit the bottom, corpses converge. They tap the side of the van like they're trying to get in. Some stand in front but I just push them over. They don't have that much balance, so it's easy to get around them when you want to.

One of the older kids is at the back door window, giving the finger to everything behind us. It makes me think of the simpler things of life we no longer have. Like road rage and traffic.

The ramp leading out of the pit is almost as steep, and I take it at a good speed. Then we're free. The kid beside me takes a deep breath, closes his eyes, and runs fingers through his hair.

The little girl comes up between us. She puts a hand on my chair and smiles out the windshield. We are free and I have all the kings of the hill with me. Now, what do I do about it?

A thought comes to my mind unbidden: They all know where I live. I slam down the accelerator and head for the gravel road.

"Hold on," I call back to the kids as I see the paved road before me. I know where we are now, and it'll take about ten minutes for me to get home.

A quick right turn on Concession 7 and I look for the Wagg Road intersection. I move fast, taking the straight road at over a hundred. There's a stop sign alert at the side of the road, one of those triangle things to tell people they will be stopping up ahead. Another waste of tax payer money.

Trees line the right side of the road, blocking the view of Highway 47. I just keep the van moving at a high speed. As we approach the intersection, several bikes rumble past. I don't slow down, but go right through the intersection, not caring what happens. A biker glances over just as I clip his back wheel. The bike wobbles comically for a few metres then tips. It slides down the road, throwing sparks everywhere. Its rider heads to the guardrail, hitting it spine first. His body folds backward and I swear I hear a loud crack.

A bike slams into the back of the van and I see the rider tumble to the ground. He's the last one in their line, so I keep speeding on Wagg.

We cross over Concession 4 without stopping. These days there's no reason to, knowing how little traffic there is. The railroad tracks rumble under the van and we keep going until Concession 3. I make a sharp left turn and start barrelling south to the house — to where Mindy is probably worried about me. Or worse, where she's lying in her own blood from a knife wound or bullet hole.

As I crest the hump to the house I see eight vehicles parked and Carl out front with his assault rifle. My heart jumps from my chest. He aims it at the van and keeps it there until I'm close. He lowers it and comes running over.

"What the fuck happened to—" His eyes go wide as he sees the kids. "Jesus, Steve!"

"We got to get in. Grab the kids. The bikers are coming."

Toasted Leather

I grab the little one who came up between the seats and hand her off to Carl. He slings the assault rifle over his shoulder and takes the kid. The oldest is already out of the van and opening the back door. He's good, shuffling them to the side of the van and making sure they follow us into the house.

The unmistakable sound of Harley motorcycles comes echoing through the air. Each of them seems to be revving their engines just to announce their arrival.

Inside the house, I wince as the breeze way door next to the garage slams shut. Cindy calls Doc over. Together they take the kids upstairs to the back TV room. Hopefully to make sure they're okay, get a little bit of the grime and smell off them. The tall kid and little girl stand there looking at me.

I motion to the staircase. "You should go upstairs. He's a doctor and the woman is like everyone's mother."

"Zoey doesn't leave me and I'm staying with you. To be safe."

I bend down, look at the little girl. The blonde curls, smudged face, and missing front tooth tell me nothing. "Can you take your friend here upstairs to the Doc?"

She lets go of his hand, steps forward, and throws her arms around me. I stand, scooping an arm under her for support. For some reason I don't think she's going to let go.

Footsteps come down the second staircase and Mindy runs toward me. I'm tackled as she hugs me and Zoey.

"You asshole! Always in trouble! Don't you leave me ever again!"

Her voice isn't harsh, but soft and distinct. I know she probably went through hell thinking of what happened to me.

"I'm okay." Nothing but a big lie, but better that then telling her how I really feelt "Here, take Zoey. Zoey, this is Mindy. She'll take care of you." I look to the big teen. "Both of you."

To my surprise, Zoey puts her arms around Mindy who frowns. "She needs a bath."

"Take her upstairs to Doc. I know he wants to give them a quick once over. They've probably been outside a long time with little to–"

A gunshot erupts and the front window's drape fluffs in like it was pushed by a breeze. I know better. It was a bullet.

Motorcycle engines rev outside, almost making the house shake. "Get them upstairs, now."

"Not the basement?" Her hand is on the door.

"Can't jump out of the basement if they set fire to the house."

Mindy takes Zoey and the other kid upstairs while Carl grabs his rifle. I always keep one inside now, easy to reach, but have been thinking of moving it out of the way when the kid comes. Now, I'm glad of my procrastination and grab the rifle leaning against the wall.

We both go into the living room in a crouch, staying behind the couch. I use the muzzle of the rifle to move the curtains aside a little only to have a bullet almost hit the end.

"Your front door. Only a few parts of clear glass and the rest etched. They won't see us looking."

Carl heads over there. I have to see what's going on outside, so I follow him.

We reach the door and look out the clear glass pane on the lower part of the window. There's only six of them. The other's must have taken the injured back to town. Pa is with them, his twin-braided beard hanging low in front of his black jacket. He's directing one of the guys to the north side of the house and another to the south. This latter one will pass right in front of the door.

"Can you open it a little?"

I think about it. "No, but there's a full sliding window in the other room." We crab walk to the other room and I slide open the window and remove the screen. Just as I lean out, a biker comes around the corner of the house. He stops, black handlebar mustache arching up at the corners as I raise my rifle. His weapon comes up as his blue eyes go wide, but I squeeze off a round before he can do anything and slip back inside.

"One down."

Carl smiles. "This is going to be expensive."

I realize what he's saying. Mindy and I have to leave this house if we're to survive. That means trying to get all we can out of this one before Pa and his gang can get past the little surprises.

"Inside the house." It's Pa's voice. "I know you took our kids. All we want is them back and for that kidnapper Steve to come out with them."

I laugh despite myself. "Funny, I thought he kidnapped me and I just saved the kids."

"Don't think so, asshole!" Carl yells.

The answer back is five shots just above where we are. They break the glass, taking out the one defence we had against the corpses at night.

"You can give us our kids and Steve, or we'll take them from ya!"

I look at Carl. "Who's upstairs?"

"Besides Doc and Cindy? Mindy and Jill. The Robertsons from up the street, and some new couple I haven't met. They did come fast when they heard you were missing."

"Jill's upstairs?" I look at the coffee table and grab the phone.

Carl glares at me. "You got a connection to the outside that we don't know about?"

"No, intercom." I hit the button and three phones buzz. One in the kitchen and two upstairs.

Jill's voice comes over the phone. "Hello?"

"Hi Jilly, miss me?"

"Like a fart in the wind." There's the sound of a clicking bolt. "I see you brought some friends."

"A dozen, but the neighborhood bullies followed us back."

"I can see that. Who's the shithead with the forked beard?"

I rub my face. "Some badass who's called Pa. Real piece of work."

"So he's the new one. Want me to take him out?"

Carl nods.

I wonder if it's possible. "Got a clean shot?"

"Maybe. He keeps poking his head around a corner, regular like clockwork. Maybe able to take him if I get the timing right."

"What about the bikes?" I keep my fingers crossed.

160

"Oh, can see almost all of them."

"Gas tanks?"

"I like how you think."

"Got a suppresser?"

"Already on."

Pa yells out again. "We want the kids and Steve. If you have them come out, we'll leave you alone."

I hear a clink. Carl smiles. "New suppressor, cancels about ninety-five percent of the rifle's noise."

Another clink, then another.

The intercom on the phone beeps at me. I turn it on.

"Three with holes."

"Pull back in," I say.

"I can get the others if I just—"

Guns go off outside. I hear the unmistakeable sound of bullets hitting my wood siding.

Carl grabs the phone. "Jill, you okay?"

"I'm okay, lover." I can hear her panting. "Pulled back just in time. Tell Steve his mattress is toast."

"Top flight of the main stairs," I tell her. "You can go prone and probably just see their feet."

"Gotcha." The phone goes silent.

Carl looks at me. "You have a plan?"

"Little bit. I buried charges in the front lawn but haven't run a line to set them off yet." I turn around, raise my head just enough to see outside. They haven't noticed the pool of gas forming in front of them. "I need my bow."

I sneak upstairs through the kitchen and find Mindy with the kids. They're in the southern room, using the thick walls and slanted room for protection. The kids are all around her, probably because they're wondering what she has under her shirt. The pregnancy is proceeding well.

The Robertsons are there, but I remember they're pretty much useless, just a young couple with no real life experience. They purchased a house up here last year after getting married because their parents told them it would be better for children. He lost his job right after and they would have lost the home if the world hadn't gone to shit. They keep coming around now, trying to figure out what to do to survive. I attract all sorts.

"My bow?" I ask, walking past Jill.

"TV room, last I saw it," Mindy calls out. "But what are you going to do with it?"

"Watch and find out." I rush into the TV room where Cindy and Doc are putting rounds into clips. My bow is to the side, a quiver of arrows beside it.

Cindy looks up. "What's going on out there?"

"Just getting ready for a barbecue. Got enough clips filled?"

Doc stops and does a count. "Twenty."

"Good." I cross over to the room I call my office. It faces the front of the house, where Jill was shooting the gas tanks from. I take out the knife, cut a little bit of curtain off and wrap it around the head of the arrow, then look out the window.

Pa is standing out front again, like nothing can hit him. Problem is one of my trees is in Jill's line of fire. She can't get a good bead on him. I open the window a few centimetres, then duck as one of the bikers starts firing my way. I'm a little trapped, but if I can just get a shot.

The biker who fired at me all of a sudden does one of those spaz dances as he falls back. Looks like Jill found a target. They all turn to the front window and start firing. We've gotten two of them and their score board is blank.

I finish wrapping the arrow head and look for something to light it with. No lighter. No nothing.

"Doc, Cindy, do either of you have a lighter? Or can one of you get to the incense box and grab that one? I need some fire."

Doc comes around to the door and gets my attention. He tosses a lighter at me then disappears. It's the one from the incense box. Hope there's fuel.

Three tries. That's how long it takes to get a flame. And once it starts to go, I hold it under the cloth wrapped arrow head. It ignites, I pull back, and stand.

I aim for the closest bike with a gas tank hole. I count to two, letting my breath flow from my body, and loose the arrow.

Three seconds pass and I think nothing will happen. Either I missed or the fire went out, or they saw it and put it out. Then a WHUSH, followed by a loud BOOM! I look out the window to see Pa riding his bike away while four bodies lay on the ground. One has a leg at an odd angle. Two have twisted bodies with bits of metal sticking out of them. Probably handle bars. The last one shakes a little before the fire finally burns the last of his life out of him. That's going to stink.

I pull the suitcase out of the closet, throw it on the bed, then open it. We'll have to leave a lot of stuff behind, but at least we can take some things with us. I start throwing clothes into it.

Mindy comes into the bedroom with Zoey still in her arms. Five of the kids follow her. "What are you doing?"

I keep packing. "We're leaving."

"Why?" She puts a hand on my shoulder.

"Because they know where we live." I return to packing. "Any time they want, they can come here and kill us. Any time. We could be sleeping and they can break in." I throw more clothes into the suitcase. "Hell, we're lucky they underestimated us just now."

"We can protect this house." Mindy grabs my arm.

"No, we can't." I pull free. "It's just a house."

"It's where we fell in love."

"And we can find another house and still be in love. But if we stay here, either they're going to shoot us, burn us, or the corpses will get us. The front window is blown. Now get the other suitcase and start putting stuff you need into it."

I think she gets it. Either that or she wants to make it seem like my idea of leaving is a good one. She puts Zoey down, and immediately the little girl starts to whimper. Mindy picks her up, then places her on the bed. This appears to be a better sacrifice to the girl and she stops the tears, for now.

"What about Sam?" Mindy asks.

"I'll get her."

"Where are we going?"

"You're coming to my place. For the time being, that is," Carl says as he enters the bedroom. He has the large boy in tow. "We can put all the kids up and then some. It won't be a bother."

"I'll take the van. Mindy, you'll take the truck." I look at the boy. "You never told me your name."

163

"Joe," he says.

"Well, Joe. Glad I got you out of there. Sorry for rushing you around."

He glances about, sees Zoey on the bed, then goes over to her, taking one dirty hand in his. "It's okay. Better to be around others than by yourself."

I can't help but notice the comfort Zoey is getting from Joe's presence. "Is Zoey your sister?"

Joe looks down at the girl. She's playing with his fingers, pulling one up and letting it drop down into her hand again. "Nope, just a lost little girl. We were the first dropped off at the shack."

Carl lifts an eyebrow. "Shack?"

I take the time to explain what the biker's did to their prisoners to soften them up. What I didn't know, Joe filled in for me. He explained how the kids bonded when some truly undesirables were left, and how they made sure they weren't victims again. The explanation of the ramp made Carl smile a bit.

"My driveway is up a little hill. Heck, most of my house is raised. I guess that's why none of the corpses come by."

Jill takes that time to walk into the room. "No, honey. The corpses keep clear of the house because of how smelly your farts are."

A small smile starts to light Joe's face and lasts for a second before disappearing. Zoey just looks up at me. "I don't like farts. They stink."

We all have a good laugh.

I throw our suitcases into the back of the van and pile the kids in. Mindy takes Zoey in the truck with Joe and the rest take their own vehicles. We're only thirty minutes clearing everything out we can take with such short notice. I vow to Mindy that we'll be back at the house as soon as the shit settles, but can't promise when that will be.

Carl and Jill lead our convoy up Concession 3, turn left on Wagg, then north on Concession 2. We take that up past Regional Road 8, and after a minute, Carl turns onto a small dirt road. There's a sign on the side of the driveway that says private property, no trespassing.

The first couple of feet on the drive are bumpy, hard on the kidneys. But then it smooths out. Sam takes that time to start howling as if the jostling causes her pain. The drive dodges left, then right, and back again, cutting off any visual from the road. Nice and secluded was what he always said when I asked where he lived.

There's a big upward dip in the drive that's only a metre high, then it levels out again. We pass a pond with a bridge to an island in its middle and then the road opens up.

If I thought Carl was just riffraff, then this changes that. The house, if you could call it that, more like a mansion to me, stands back from the trees only ten metres. It sits in a cleared area with a pond almost the size of my property. There's a three car garage attached to the building and I see the glint of a solar roof. I remember Carl said he has power here.

The grass looks freshly mowed and the hedges near the water nice and neat. The taxes alone must be more than I make in a year. One of the garage doors opens and Carl drives right in, just like he owns the place. I stop near the front door and put the van into park. The kids are out faster than I can undo my seat belt.

Mindy pulls up beside me, her eyes wide. She rolls down the window. "Jill told me he lived in a big house but I never imagined."

The front door opens and Jill steps out, a beer in each hand, Carl follows close behind her. He holds two glasses. They both make their way over to the vehicle just as Mindy climbs down.

"This is for you." He holds out the glass and I take it. "And this is for you." The next glass appears full of water. He then takes the other beer off Jill. "Welcome to your new home."

Sam wails in the van.

Carl throws another log on the fire, then comes back to the couch. He sits, picks up his beer, and takes a good swig.

The inside of the house is huge. Two stories, a dozen bedrooms, and five bathrooms. It's laid out nicely and the way it flows tells me someone paid a lot of money to get it this way.

All the furniture matches the rooms. Nothing stands out as gaudy or not belonging to the place. Everything has a function. His power wall contains five banks, each just finishing their charge to one hundred percent. I figure even in a downpour they'd charge with the roof he has. And the furnace, such a lovely state-of-the-art geothermal unit. All self-sustaining. The envy must be apparent, for on the way back to the main living room, Carl tells me about his parents, and how they ran five of the pits in the area.

Mindy and Jill take the kids for bathing while Carl tells me about the home. He's proud, but not pretentious. More humble than I've ever seen him. And now that I know what he's like and where he comes from, I get a better understanding of why Jill wants to be with him. He's a good guy.

By the end of the tour, the kids are being washed with new clothes laid out for them to wear. Each gets a room assigned, and Carl and I go outside to enjoy the fresh air as Sam meows for something to eat. That's when I spy the smoke column reaching into the sky from where we came and I drop my glass.

Dirt and Burgers

Carl spins me around before I get to the van and I shift to take a swing at him. He backs away, hands up. There's no one else around us. The sun is sinking, shadows lengthening. We'll need to turn on lights soon, especially if we drive anywhere. Probably what the bikers want, us to come back to the house, try to save what's there, then follow us back to where we're hiding. I get it, and Carl just wants to make sure I don't do it.

After some hesitation, I look at my fist, then lower it. There's no reason to fight. This is my friend. My buddy. We work well together, and to hit him could ruin that silent agreement, the *I've got your back* that's between us.

I look at the ground, heat rising to my cheeks. "I'm sorry. Sorry for being an idiot."

Carl just gives his head a little shake. "Nothing I wouldn't have done in your shoes." He heads back to the porch. "Come on, buy you another drink."

I follow him, find the remnants of the shattered glass and bend over to start picking it up.

Carl places a hand on my shoulder. "Don't worry about it. We'll clean it later." He takes a deep breath. "We need to tell the girls about this."

I straighten up, wonder when he became so insightful, and follow him into the house. There's nothing to say or do out here. He's right. Just let the girls know our home is now gone. We'll make them pay.

Zoey runs down the stairs, naked and dripping wet. Some of the dirt is washed away, while other parts of her are still covered in grime. Carl scoops her up as she passes.

We head upstairs and into a large bathroom, a tub in the centre is filled with children. Mindy is helping clean the girls as best as she can. Carl hands Zoey over to Jill with a smile.

"Looks like you lost something."

She takes the girl and dumps her into the bath with the others. "Now stay in there until you're clean."

I look around. "Where're the boys?"

"In the other room," Jill says, applying a liberal amount of soap on Zoey's hair.

"We'll check up on them," Carl says, and nods to the hall.

Once outside I turn to him. "Thought we were going to tell them."

"Not right now, not with the kids." Carl leads me down the hall to another room and opens the door.

The boys are all sitting in a huge hot tub. The water bubbles as the jets scrub them free of dirt. Even Joe is sitting in the tub, letting the water wash over him.

The back wall, made of glass bricks, lets in light from the evening sun. It's a wonderful effect, until Carl speaks.

"Shit, I'm going to have to drain that now."

The kids just stare at him, then Joe starts to stand.

"Don't." I hold out my hand and Joe stops. "You just sit right down there, young man. It's time to become civilized again."

Carl smiles at the group. "I'm getting burgers out, who wants one?"

They all stand and raise their hands shouting, "Me!"

We both smile, make motions to quiet down and sit. Carl starts to move out of the room but stops.

"You'll need to be clean to get a burger, so wash up really good before coming outside."

Carl and I stand on the patio watching the burgers cook on his grill. It's a simple thing, just brick and a cooking surface with a little fire log catch below. I find it ingenious to make something so simple yet so thought provoking as a wood fire. Everything tastes better when cooked over real wood flames and embers. Some people swear by charcoal while others say gas, but wood is the ultimate slow cook.

It appears Carl is also a survivalist with a good store of food and other supplies. We talk about what he's done to make the house more efficient and his plans before the world went to hell. There's something of a kindred spirit about us that grows even brighter.

I have another drink, thanks to Carl, and this time it's in a plastic glass. I said nothing when he poured it. Guess I deserve that one. And now we wait for the meat to cook.

"Shit!" Carl says. "Forgot the buns."

"I don't think the kids will mind."

He glances at me. "No, but Jill will. Can you go into the freezer and pull out two dozen, just in case."

"Sure." I get up. "Anything else?"

"There's pickles in the basement lauder along with other stuff. Grab two onions and tomatoes as well, will you?" He flips a burger. "Best to cover all the bases."

"No problem."

I head to the basement. It's a large one, and the water pump hammers away like mad to keep the pressure up. Not much more to see here, just a poured concrete floor and five metal posts scattered about to hold the house up. His geothermal unit is huge. Pipes run from it to the north wall. Five rows of ten twelve-volt batteries on the south wall show a trickle of a drain on the resources. With those at full, he could probably power the house for a few days of darkness.

The pickles are easy to find, just jars upon jars of the things on a shelf. He must like them or something. It only takes a minute to find everything needed, then back to the yard. I'm surprised to see Joe already there, washed and clean. He's wearing one of Carl's many Hawaiian shirts and a pair of shorts way too big for him. He's trying to keep them up by holding the loops with one hand. The sight is something funny, but I try to keep my amusement to a minimum.

One by one the boys trickle out. Carl gets the buns thawed and gives them burgers. I don't think they even taste them let alone don't eat their own fingers as well. Only one doesn't want a second burger, but that could be because he's only about five.

The girls' faces light up at the sight of the food. Carl's a champ, feeding them first and wanting until they're all full before dishing out food for the rest of us.

"This is going to put a big dent in my supplies." He scans the kids.

169

"Think we can talk some of the others into adopting a few of them?"

"The Robertsons' would take two," I say while chewing. It gets me a nasty look from Mindy. "Boy and girl I would think. Have to find two who won't drive them insane. They're a young couple."

"We'll adopt Joe and Zoey," Mindy says. "They're bonded like brother and sister, so I don't want them to be split up."

Carl nods. "That's four of the twelve. We'll adopt two as well." He frowns.

Jill puts a hand on his arm. "What's wrong?"

"I hate breaking the kids up," he says. "It's like we're telling them we don't want them around."

I glance down to the small pond the kids are playing near. They seem happy to be together here, but is it too much? "I don't think they'll be too concerned about it. They're kids, and resilient. Besides, none of us could ask you to shoulder the burden alone."

Carl nods. "And what about you guys? You need a place to stay. I can let you live here, but then the four of us would be under foot all the time. Do you want to have your own place?"

Mindy glances at me. "With the baby coming, it would be good to have our own place again."

I stiffen. "Mindy, the bikers torched the house."

There's something in her eye, but she wipes at it quickly. "We'll find another."

"My property is big," Carl says. "We could build a foundation just over there"–he points to the small clearing just south of his house–"and it would be nothing to take one of those prefabs off the lot on 48."

I think about it for a second. "It would take a lot of time. Building the foundation would take a month at least."

"I'm not doing anything special for the next little while." Carl grins. "Besides, it would be nice to have you right here if we need to do a raid or something."

"We'll need a back hoe."

"And a dozer."

"Cinder blocks."

"Lots of cement."

"Have to drill for a well also."

Carl smiles. "There's a well drilled there already, just have to tie into it."

Mindy waves to get our attention. "What are these houses like you're talking about?"

"We'll have to show you," Carl says. "It'll have to happen late, so spying eyes can't see what we're up to." He winks and nods toward the girls and kids.

I lower the binoculars and hand them over to Carl. He takes them, wiggles up a little higher on my backyard neighbour's roof, and looks out. There's not much left of my house.

We can see right onto the property and then some, but nothing tugged more at my heart than the image of a charred skeleton where my home once stood. I think of the one wall that survived from the initial blacksmith shop built in the 1800's. An irreplaceable piece of history, gone forever because some bikers wanted to play. They don't know what they've done.

"I don't see Pa," Carl says.

"No, but I bet he's there." I take back the binoculars and stare out at the home. Movement catches my eye and I spy one of the lookouts. He's sitting near my fire pit, smoking. The bastard even built a fire back there.

The early April air holds a slight chill and the sky is threatening to open up on us at any time. Dark, almost black, clouds lumber across the sky toward the South-East. A sure sign of spring. Carl suggested a little outing to scout for supplies, little did I know this included checking out the old home.

"Want to have a little fun?" He unslings his hunting rifle and screws on the suppressor.

"How silent is that thing?"

"Pretty silent." He aims, adjusts the sights. "From where we are, those monkeys down there won't even hear anything except their buddy falling."

I think of all the lives they've taken from us. Just last week they raided a family past concession 4, burned down the home and raped the woman and her three daughters. Not something pleasant. Only this time, we were almost ready for them. Carl got four of them, I got the other two. I think he has some real hate for rapists.

"Just take out the one by the fire pit. No one else. Make them wonder. It's a nice message to tell them we can touch them any time we want to."

"Good idea." Carl readjusts, takes a slow breath in, holds it, and lets it out slow. Before half of the breath is out, the familiar pop of the rifle sounds. He's right, the suppressor makes his shot all but silent.

There's a spray of fine red mist in front of the biker and he falls to his knees, then face plants in the snow. "No head shot?"

"Not this time. They'll find him and hopefully he'll have changed by then. They'll need to shoot him again."

It's an interesting psychological ploy. Make them do the kill shot on someone already dead. They'll know we did it, and let the guy change. Then they may look a little differently at their friends, wondering who could kill who. Nice plan.

"Let's get out of here." Carl starts to back down the roof.

Joe waves goodbye to the last boy leaving the house. I watch as our new son drops his head and stares at the ground. "What's wrong?"

He turns from me and starts to walk away.

"Joe, if something is bothering you—"

"Why did he have to leave?"

"There's not enough here for everyone." I stand. "If he stayed, we'd be out of food and such much quicker than planned."

He turns to me. "No, why did my dad leave?"

I scramble for something to say. "I don't know." The kid gets a distant look in his eyes. "Maybe you should tell me about it."

Joe comes to the bed and sits down. He stares at the wall for a bit. "Mom said Dad had to leave. And when the bikers came, I wasn't strong enough to save her. Dad could have. Why did he leave?"

"That depends." I put my arm around his shoulders. "Sometimes parents fall out of love with each other. Sometimes one does something absolutely unforgivable, other times they die." I take a deep breath. "He probably needed to leave in order to be a better person."

"He never came back."

"Was he in the forces?"

"I don't think so." Joe stares off into the distance.

"Did he wear a uniform?"

"I can't remember."

"It was that long ago?"

He stares at the floor. "I think I was five."

"It's hard to tell why a man would leave a wife and child. If he worked for the military, he could have been deployed, maybe even killed. Didn't your mom talk about him?"

"No, it's just that... I took care of those kids, and now they're all gone, just like my dad. I'll never see them again."

That's the ticket; he's depressed because he thinks they're gone for good. "You will. They're not that far away, and when the bikers are all cleared out—"

His laugh has no humour in it. "They'll never leave."

It doesn't take long for me to learn how to use the back hoe. I have a good amount done on the foundation and want to finish it but Carl and Joe are racing toward me and waving their hands. Curiosity gets me. I stop and take a swig out of my canteen.

The noonday sun is warming up the mid-April day and I shut off the machine to find out what the problem is.

They stop just in front of me and jump off their quads. Carl gives Joe a high five and they step up to the side of the machine. Carl leans against it and Joe folds his arms like nothing is going on. I wait for one of them to speak.

"Looks like you got a lot done," Carl says, motioning to the foundation I'm digging.

"Yeah, little bit." I lean forward. "What's up?"

"I'll have to even it out once you're finished but we can work with this."

Joe grins at him. Carl is stalling, something he likes to do before springing big news. It's gotta be good news this time from the way he's jabbering on.

"Found a dozer that'll do the leveling really good. We can make a walk out for you and Mindy and Joe real easy."

"Give."

"Give what?" Carl glances at Joe and they both shrug. "There's nothing to say. We found the dozer and thought it would be good for you to hear about it. That and the corpses are migrating north right now."

"Yeah, the dozer is good news and the corpse are fine…" It hits me. The corpses are migrating north. I'm right about their behaviour. "You said the corpses are going north?"

"Yeah," Joe says. "It seems like a lot of them got stuck in Whitby during the winter and froze. Now that they're free, most are just walking north."

I smile. "The biker's fence."

"Yeah," Carl says. "The biker's fence."

Doc's penetrating stare hits each one of use and we all shut up one at a time. The gray hair on his face reminds us he's much older and wiser than the rest of what he calls *young kids* all around him.

Our little community has grown. The twenty went down to sixteen, then up to forty. We each have a voice, but Doc makes sure no one runs rickshaw over anyone else. He's a firm task master, but fair.

"Look people, we need to get this sorted out, and not go off half-cocked like most want to." He points to Carl. "Go ahead, tell us what you saw."

Carl stands. "Yesterday, me and Joe were scouting south, looking for new places to find goods we don't have. As you know, there's a lot of little farms that have fresh fruit and veg growing."

"Get to the point," Doc growls.

"Sure." He wipes his lip. "Well, we made it as far south as Claremont, just to see if we could find something in the stores there. A little past Central Street we ran into a lot of corpses. They're all heading north, just like Steve predicted."

The young Robertson man stood up. "But what good is that?"

I stand up. "It means all the corpses that didn't make it south because of the lake are now heading north, and through our area."

People started to rumble at that pronouncement. "That's not good."

"I don't want to leave my home because of corpses."

"What're we going to do?"

The voices boil up again and Doc slams his hand on his lap to get attention once again. "Carl, Steve, I know you two wouldn't have those shit-eatin' grins on your faces if this wasn't good news. So out with it. What does this do for us?"

Carl grins wider. "Steve and I have scouted the bikers fence, and it's

174

basically a funnel with no opening at the top. All the corpses will move north, hit the fence, and start to fill up. Once they can't move north again, they'll start to wander around like they usually do." He's smiling now. "So, just imagine the bikers' surprise as the corpses come up through their little town. Not just a few of them, but probably thousands. They'll be overrun in no time."

"What's stopping them from cutting the fence and letting them out?" I recognize Cindy's voice in that question.

"Only us." Carl picks up his sniper rifle. "And the crack shots we've become."

Missing

The bikers did a number of things smart. They took over the town, squashed anyone who stood in their way, and tried to protect themselves from the hordes travelling south. The fence, something of a strange thing for us, stretches out from Concession 5 and Regional Road 8 in an arc with the apex at Ball Road and Centre Road. It then curves back down to highway 47 and Lakeridge Road. A massive eight kilometres across the top of Uxbridge. How they got it up so fast and along such a wide area is beyond me. They must have scavenged every shop for kilometres to get that much chain link, but they did it.

Carl and I are at either end of the fence, guarding what we think will be a mass exodus from the town. We have no idea when the corpses will get here, but they will. And it's up to us to make sure the bikers don't escape. I imagine they'll come out in a hurry, no organized march, just chaos. And we don't know if it'll be today or tomorrow, but it will happen. The only thing we can do is stand watch and make sure none of them get out. And we've taken a page from their book to help.

Several of us spent days putting together nail caltrops just like the ones they used. Nasty, but it'll work to stop them dead in their tracks. We've also dug some short pits and stuck tree limbs into them. Of course we sharpened the points to add a little more to the surprise. I just wish we had more time to get things prepared.

From the speed and distance, we calculated today or tomorrow the horde would hit the bottom of the town, but being sure is like playing the lottery, the only correct way is to not play the odds. So we wait. Hope that today will be the day. My ass is sore from sitting behind the trees. At least we could have brought more comfortable chairs, but no, we had to use the one's that would keep us awake.

There's a culvert running a good length of both roads, so I'm not too worried about any corpses coming up behind me. They'll make a lot of racket before it's too late. Likewise, if anyone approaches by vehicle, or any other way, I'll hear them. It's just one of the perks for getting picked first for this type of duty.

I have a good, unobstructed view for most of the area, but some trees do block a little of the approach. They're across from the pond and I'm not too worried about it.

A stretch and yawn, then I reach down for the thermos to get some tea. One cup, that's all I need for now. And when I look up with it in my hand, there's a corpse coming out of the forest. I put the tea down and pick up my rifle. The scope allows a good look at the creature. It lumbers forward, most of the skin on one leg is rotten away, probably from the winter thaw. I see a distinct limp, the cloudy eyes searching the distance without finding what they're hunting for.

I zoom in on another corpse in the field to the east; it walks almost without issues, following a path that only it knows. Without waiting any more, I pick up my gear and move to the other side of Regional Road 8 and setup up a new spot in a field. Probably a sod farm, but now just a field of dirt and mud.

Once comfortable, I finish my tea, and wait for someone to come and try to cut the fence.

The sound of a quad coming across the field breaks me from the trance of watching corpses try to push their way through the fence. They are so singularly minded, or maybe they see me and just want to eat. There must be about thirty of them now, all different shapes and sizes in various states of decay. It won't be long until all of them have rotted down to just bones and sinews.

I recognize the driver after a few minutes, it's the young Robertson, and he's taking his time getting to the spot. In fact, after checking the time, he's a little early. Not sure why, it's a beautiful late April day. Little on the chilly side, but still nice.

He pulls up, removes his helmet, and smiles.

"Nice day for protecting a fence, I see." He stares at the corpses.

"Looks like about forty there."

"Probably only thirty."

He glances around. "Where's your quad?"

"Carl's picking me up in a few minutes. Thought it best to just bring one, knowing we're at the same place." Rock Star, or the corpse I started calling that because of the Boston T-shirt it wears, pushes an arm through the links. Most of the flesh is gone, and bone thrusts out as if he's trying to wave me over.

"That's sick," Robertson says.

"Yeah." I fold my chair. "But there's worse coming, I'm sure of it. The majority of the corpses will be either rotted or decayed enough by next year that we're not going to have to worry about them. Then it's just making sure everyone who dies doesn't come back."

"I wonder how many people survived the initial outbreak?"

It's a question I've asked myself a number of times. "Hard to tell. With how fast it all started, I'm sure very few got out of the big cities in time. I'd say maybe one in twenty survived the initial infection stage and then we lost twenty to thirty percent more over the year while people starved because of lack of food. Not many hunter-gathers left in our society. Heck, most of us living out here have been lucky to get away with our lives."

Robertson glances at me. "Mostly thanks to you, Carl, and Doc. If it wasn't for your help at the start, we would have all died."

"Just doing what every good person would." I start scanning the east, looking for Carl's quad. "We all have to look out for each other."

"Not everyone thinks that way." He takes out binoculars, starts to scan the fence line. "You ever taken a good look at the corpses?"

"No."

"Some of them are interesting."

"Don't want to start thinking of them as people," I say. "If you do, then hesitation sets in when you have to put one down. It's not pretty what happens to people who hesitate."

"I can imagine."

We wait; him for something to happen and me for Carl to come and pick me up. He's one of those people who are always late unless someone stands over them to make sure they're on time. Hard to believe he runs – I mean ran – a successful company before this happened.

I look at my watch, concern tracing a line across my brow. "You have any idea what could be keeping him?"

Robertson stops counting the corpses. "Isn't he always late? Like, one of those who'd be late for his own funeral types?"

"He's over thirty minutes late." I get it. Carl's tendency is well-known so maybe he's shooting the shit with someone. "I'll give him another fifteen."

When forty-five minutes runs past I become really concerned.

"Can I borrow your quad? I want to check on Carl to see what's taking him so long."

"Sure, should be gassed up." I've never heard him say anything but yes to any of my requests.

The keys are still in the ignition. His quad is a little different than mine, but I get the feel of the automatic transmission in no time. It flies across the field and I stick to the fence line just to make sure I don't miss Carl. There's one of us every two klicks, and when I stop to ask if anyone's seen my friend they all answer no. It could be the concern on my face or the anxiousness of my question, but they all try to make light of it, pointing out Carl would be late for his own funeral.

I keep moving along, looking for the one who protects my back.

As I pass Centre Road, the fence starts to fill up with corpses, all of them pushing against it. I'm surprised it holds, even with the braces we put in place, but it does.

The arc toward Lake Ridge Road goes through a small residential area just south of the correctional facility. The building stands empty, probably because the bikers pulled everyone from there.

I stop at the last guard before Carl's location. Jim something. Never been good with names.

"Seen Carl?"

He scratches his head, eyes look over my shoulder a little. "Nope, not been here, but I only just got here about an hour ago. Isn't he watching the end?"

The corpses have thinned out once again, like they're all congregating in the centre for some unknown reason. I watch as some of them walk with jerky movements to the west.

"Yeah, he was supposed to pick me up."

Jim just shrugs.

I hit the gas and speed across the field to my last destination, Carl's post.

The Uxbridge town sign stands there, unmarked by the past winter, and Carl's quad sits under it along with another I don't recognize. It would be his relief, but where either of them are, I don't know.

A few corpses have missed the fence's end and mill about nearby. I unsling my rifle and shoot them, relying on my suppressor to keep the curious ones from realizing what I'm doing.

There's nothing special about the quads. They're the ones we took from the dealership before winter. Even after the hard usage we put them through they still have a shine on them.

I count just over a dozen corpses caught behind the fence and a few more of them wandering the golf course on the other side. Guess the bikers wanted to have an unobstructed play field.

With the quad fired back up, I make my way down the road, toward a planter made out to look like a well. Its small peaked roof is a little more worn than before, and the scrub growing inside it reminds me of wild flowers. I pass the freshly shot corpses and stop at the driveway.

The gravel appears freshly disturbed, making me wonder what caused it. I get off the quad and examine the ground up close. Drag marks and ATV tracks. I jump back on the quad and follow the tracks up the gravel road until it turns into dirt. There's a line of trees that come up to the road and I stop before it; there's a house just beyond them. Times like these it pays to be cautious and I need to remind myself that I'm no good to anyone if something bad happens to me.

I can see very little from the small line of trees. A slow sneaking jog brings me to the edge of a pond, just behind a large maple. Still nothing, but I do see two quads parked in the grass near the house. One is beat up while the other looks like the twin to mine. There's no one in sight, so I half crouch and make my way to the next tree, check again, then to a small forested section of the property to the west.

Dodging between the trees with no worry about being seen is easier than being in the open trying to find cover. The trees take me right up to the house, just above the empty pool. There're corpses in it instead of water, and they just stand there, eyes watching the deck and not moving.

The treeline takes me within spitting distance of the house. There's a large patio door looking out to the pool. Two figures move about inside and I can make out what appears to be Pa and Joe. I stop. My mind flies through everything I know. Joe, the kid Mindy and I adopted from the group. He stands there with Pa, the head of the biker gang. Things I never thought of being strange start to fall into place. The little things like how he was better off than the other kids. Times he took off for a day on a quad only to return it full. Just little things, but unexplained. And how he never talked bad about the bikers.

They're talking, or what appears to be talking. Joe has a bottle in his hand, and as he lifts it up and takes a swig, I know its beer. Maybe he's older than he said, maybe he's not. There's no way of knowing, not now with the world gone to shit.

I make a dash toward the back wall of the house, then flatten against it. Over to the other side of the patio door I see two pairs of feet sticking out. Here are my missing people, but there's no way of being sure unless I can see them.

Voices come from the house and I can just make them out. I slink over to the patio door, keeping under the window while I approach. Once by it, a simple reach over and give it a soft push to open it a little more for me to hear.

"… but I did get information for you."

Joe's voice. I can tell that seventeen-year-old squeak and approval-needing tone anywhere.

"It was a good plan. I'm surprised he went for it," Pa says.

"Worked well."

A few seconds later, Pa says, "What happened?"

"I kind of like him."

"Which one, Carl or Steve?"

"Both," Joe says after a few seconds. "They treated me real nice. But they're not family."

"No, they're not."

The patio door slides open.

My first thought is to attack whoever comes through, but there's a chance of not surviving. It takes a second, but I dash toward the corner of the house closest to me. It's the best hiding place I can think of.

Pa steps through, followed by Joe. They haven't seen me yet, so there's still time to make my way out of the area. That wouldn't serve anyone, so I edge to the corner and unsling my rifle. I could get one, but probably not both.

Taking out Pa would be the best bet to get rid of the bikers. To miss this chance would be a crime. I centre the sight on him. The bulk on his body means armour. A good clean head shot, that's what I'll need. But he won't stop moving.

Pa walks to the other side of the house, out of sight. The sound of someone hitting something like a wet bag rings out, then Pa is dragging someone from the side toward the pool. His jerky movements make it impossible to get a perfect bead, and I'll only have one shot.

He drags the body, kicking and screaming, toward the diving board, and gets up on it. With a knife at the throat, the man stops struggling, and his eyes go wide as he sees the reaching hands of corpses.

Pa is talking to the man. I can see his mouth moving, but they are too far away for me to hear the soft voice he uses when talking to people he has in his grasp. The scene stretches out. Pa talking and the man either shaking his head or nodding. I know what he's saying, just the same thing he said to me a few months ago. Elastics.

I still have no shot. Pa's holding the man. If I kill him, there's a chance the man will go in with him. Then I recognize the victim. One of our people. The one who was supposed to relieve Carl. Mike, or Mark. Something like that. I hate trying to remember names.

Pa spins him around, makes him sit on the diving board, kicks his legs over the side, then steps back until he's on the concrete deck with Joe by his side. He then takes out a gun and shoots Mark's foot.

The scream echoes through me and strangles my soul. Mark slumps forward, almost rolls until scrambling to stay on the board.

Joe hands Pa a large wrench.

"I would like an answer," he yells. "You have another foot."

"I told you, I don't know where Steve is!"

Pa fires again, hitting Mark in the ankle of the same foot. Another scream hammers against me. I aim, but Joe's head gets in the way. I try to will him to take a step to the left, out of my line of fire.

Joe throws his beer bottle into the pool. "I think they're hungry, Pa."

"Get us another beer," Pa says in a load voice. He bends over. Now his head is hidden by his body.

Joe walks into the house.

"One of the great things about this pool that I found out a few months ago is that the bolts holding this board are loose."

He starts to work on something and Mark screams at him not to do it. The board dips a little.

"See, loose."

Pa stands up and I take aim at him. One slow, deep breath, hold it, then start to let it out. Before I squeeze the trigger, Joe is back in the way.

He hands Pa a beer and opens his own. "We should just kill him. It's been a long time since I've had fresh meat."

Joe takes out a large knife and I remember what the driver had said to me all those months ago. The kids may eat me.

My finger itches on the trigger, eye is focused on Pa's head. I squeeze. The rifle lets out a crack as the bullet races toward its target.

Reunion

As the sight comes down from the recoil of the rifle, I see nothing but air. He must be dead. I open my other eye, move away from the scope, and see Pa bending over the slumped body of Joe. How did I shoot the kid? Maybe he moved just as I squeezed the trigger. It's possible he saw the rifle sticking out of the grass and walked toward it just at the right time. I don't know. What I do know is Pa is very distraught over the kid being hit. So I stand. I want to go over and check on him. Make sure Joe is okay, not dead. But something tells me to focus on the moment. What's done is done. Joe was a spy for the biker gang to find out things about me. Shit! A spy.

The biker stands, hands dripping with blood. He must see me, for his .45, is out of its holster and in his hand fast. Pa takes two steps forward, brows furrowed, and starts to fire.

I duck behind the wall as a bullet strikes the ground right where my head had been. There's no time to think. I will my legs to work and thank life they do. Up, run. Not toward the trees, that'll put me in his line of fire. Around the house. If I'm lucky, he'll keep coming this way, thinking I came from the north. He'll follow me, and I can come around back to the pool.

There's no one at the front of the house, so I keep running, trying to make it as fast as possible. A scream splits the air. It's the same scream Mark let out when Pa shot him, only this one gargles out into death.

I round the next corner of the house, come up to the rear of the building, and look around it. Mark isn't on the diving board any more, but Carl is against the wall, trying to sit up. His face is bloodied, one eye all but swollen shut. His bottom lip is split on the side, and there're several cuts on his face as if he's been beaten.

He braces against the wall as I round the corner, probably thinking I'm Pa or something. Shoulders visibly relax, he pushes to his feet, but stumbles forward.

"Where are you, Steve?" Pa calls out from somewhere on the other side of the house. "I'm sure it's you."

"Who the fuck was that?" Carl says.

I rush over to him. "Pa, the one I told you about."

"Come out, Steve. I'll make it easy for you." Pa's voice sounds distant, as if he's yelling while facing away. I can only hope he's looking in the trees for me. It's the place I would have hidden if not for Carl and Mark.

"He's fucked up."

I step behind Carl. My knife makes quick work of the bindings.

Carl turns to face me. "Well, what now?"

I slip my knife into its sheath. "Not sure. You have any idea where your weapons are?"

The rumbling of Harleys with no mufflers sounds in the distance. As if anything else could go wrong.

"Only thing I remember is Joe coming over and saying you wanted to get going soon." He wipes his mouth and flinches. "Thought it was funny he just didn't take you home. Mark and I were just talking a little. I turned my back and then all went black."

"Joe's dead." I pull out my glock and hand it to Carl.

"Joe?" He takes the weapon and cocks it.

"He was working with Pa." I hand him two clips.

"Fuck." He puts the clips into a side pocket. "Think any of the other kids are working with that son of a bitch?"

The sound of bikes gets closer. They'll be coming up the drive soon.

"No, don't think so." I point to the line of trees just south of the house and behind the pond. "My quad's there. Think you can get to it?"

"Try and stop me." He takes off at a limping run, favouring his right leg. It's not a bee line, more like a little curve. I hold back, not wanting to show him how injured he is.

"Steve, you killed my boy," Pa's voice sounds closer.

I glance around the corner but he's not there.

The unmistakable explosion of a .45 punches through the air. I look over and see Carl fall to the ground.

"Carl!" I inadvertently take one step forward.

"Steve?" Pa says.

My attention turns to him. The man is only one step past the edge of the house but his eyes burn as they take me in. Blood spatters smear his leather jacket, eyes red rimmed.

I spin, taking off at a dead run around the house. Dust clouds plume on the dirt driveway toward us. I need to get out of here before they arrive.

A shot echoes out as a bullet cuts the air where I was a moment ago. I run toward the trees to the north, hoping to get there before Pa can round the house. As I sprint behind a tree, wood splitters off it as a bullet cracks the oak. I keep going.

The woods thicken. I glance around and cannot see Pa or anyone following. The bikers are all at the house now.

I run west, and then south to double around and head back toward my quad. And hopefully to safety.

Three of the sentry posts are vacant except for their quads. I come up on the fourth only to find one of our people riddled with bullets. Not one through the head. My stomach empties at the sight. One of my bullets makes sure he's not coming back. I can't even remember his name, just that we called him Red. Did he have a family?

I take a scattered route back to Carl's house, hoping to get people together in order to call up the troops. We need everyone ready for the threat. These bikers need to pay. Every house I pass is either ablaze or ashes. No one's around for me to call upon.

The gas gage on the quad shows a quarter left. I gun the engine, push the bike on the gravel and through the different areas in a desperate hope to find someone, anyone, to help take on the bikers. No one is around, no sign of what happened besides the torched homes. I even stop at one, the Robertsons' home.

They picked a home just south of Carl's place, not knowing we lived up the street. It takes only a few minutes to climb up their driveway.

I take a deep breath as a white van comes into view. The sides are dented. The old 80's style vehicle looks more utilitarian than anything if it wasn't for the bondo patched rust and busted break lights. There's something not right about the image, for the Robertsons would never drive a cargo van with the kids.

A window explodes outward, sending shards of glass into the air. Smoke billows out of the opening and the front door bursts open. Collette Robertson runs out, eyes wide, screaming. She sees me and makes a bee line directly toward me.

"Get back here, bitch!" A large dark-haired man wearing a biker's leather jacket and chaps strides out of the house. His long gray hair billows out behind him, pant's belt still undone. He's struggling to do it up while chasing the woman and yelling.

I unsling my rifle and chamber a round. The biker stops, reaches into his jacket, and brings out a revolver. I'm faster. The rifle barks and the biker takes a step back. Red swells on his chest. I fire another round, taking off the side of his head.

Collette grabs the front of my quad, her voice shrill as she screams. "The kids, they're all in on it."

An explosion rumbles through the air and the rest of the windows blow out.

"Get on!" I yell over the noise, mouth filling with grit.

She climbs onto the back of the quad and grabs me around the middle. A quick gun of the engine and we speed down the road to home.

I don't know what to expect. There's something in my mind telling me that we're okay, safe from prying eyes. That no one really knows where we live, expect, Joe knew. He's lived with us for a few months, came and went at his leisure, with no one questioning where he drove the quad.

We hit the driveway at sixty klicks. Gravel flies and a dust trail kicks up.

I round the dogleg. Three vans are parked in front of the house, their back doors are open, and Zoey sits cowering in the back of the closest one.

"We have to go!" Collette says.

I don't hear her, just zero in on Zoey. Buy why? If she's part of the gang, then somehow they would be using her. They are not. My mind is made up quick, and I get off the quad and run to the van.

Once at the door, I can see Zoey is balling.

"Zoey!" I cry out.

Her big blue eyes grow wide as she stares at me. She jumps up and runs forward. Her little arms circle my neck and a small voice whispers, "They have Mindy."

The world spins.

Zoey sits between Colette and me on the quad. I see smoke rising up over the trees from the place we started to call home just a few weeks ago. We're running again, but I have an idea where we'll be safe, or as safe as we possibly can in a world upside down and totally fucked up.

I turn onto Aurora Road and then Island Lake Drive. Once at the end we head into the forest between two homes with circular driveways. The pine trees whip at us as we pass.

We break out into a small field. A fence circles part of the clearing and corpse's mill about, flesh all but falling from their bony arms. I try not to look. Keep concentrating on the forest before us.

The trees reach skyward, new buds of leaves just starting to form. Trunks speed past us. Then a field, shrubs dotting it. I slow, maneuver the quad around a few stray trees, and head for the boathouse between the small pond and lake. The quad comes to a stop, gas completely empty.

Colette grabs my shoulder. "Where are we?"

"Shadow lake camp." I climb off the quad.

"What are we going to do here?"

I lift Zoey off the quad. "Hide while we figure out what's happening."

"What about—"

I turn to her. "Fuck, Colette, give me a few minutes."

She closes her mouth and gets off the quad.

With a firm hold on Zoey, I walk past the boat house and toward the small outfitter building. No shadows move inside it, but that's not my destination. The house just south is the target. Several trees surround the home on three sides, leaving the northern face free of obstruction. I walk up to the front door, turn the handle, and walk inside. Collette follows close behind.

The house is empty but secure. No smell of rotting corpses, no unbathed people, nothing but fresh baked bread. I climb the stairs, find a bedroom, walk into it, and lay Zoey on the bed. The room hasn't changed from last I saw it.

"You need to rest. I need to rest."

Zoey looks up at me with doe eyes. "Where's Mindy?"

"I don't know." It drives a knife in me to say it. A realization hits that the woman I love is not with me anymore and still carrying my unborn child. Taken by bikers who eat flesh. My mind wonders but snaps back before going to the one place I don't want it to. Zoey is still staring at me. "But we'll find her. Soon. I promise."

The kid is strong, I know that, but tears still try to well up in her eyes. Before I can say anything else, she rolls over, presenting me with her back, head in pillow. She did that to me one day when I made her clean the room she had. Didn't talk to me for a week. I know this as being a "leave me alone" move she does when there's nothing more she wants to say.

"Get some sleep, sweetheart. We'll figure out what to do in the morning." I give her shoulder a squeeze and leave the room.

I sit on the porch of the house, a bottle of some cut-rate scotch beside me, cap removed, and a third of the drink no longer there. My gut burns. Cheap scotch.

The sun casts shadows across the pond as it sets. I watch as fish jump to catch spring bugs. The early years of hunting and fishing with my father come to mind, and I let myself get lost in the memory. Anything but to think about what's happening to Mindy.

Collette sits down beside me; one hand reaches out and takes the bottle. She stares at it for a few moments, then takes a swig.

"It's shit."

She coughs, puts the bottle down. "Yes, it is."

We stare out at the pond, each absorbed in our own thoughts. But what I want to think about is far away, beyond my grasp. And yet, I can remember her, the gentleness of her eyes and smile. And yet, she is lost.

As the sun sets past the trees, the temperature plummets. Soon it becomes too much for me to bear. I stand, grab the bottle, and walk into the house. The couch looks just as comfortable as anything, so I lay down on it and let sleep take me.

DOUGLAS OWEN

I don't sleep well, but toss and turn all night, waking every few minutes just to try and allow slumber to come once again. Nothing really helps. I used to use antacids to help calm my stomach, but since bad scotch is just that, and the end of civilization is upon us…

I open my eyes. A sliver of light enters the east window through the trees. Just enough to illuminate the old face staring down at me and scowling. Her eyes hide behind glaring lids covered in wrinkles, just like the rest of her face. The short white curly hair is thin. She straightens, glances to the floor where I left the scotch, and shakes her head.

"You never could hold your liquor, Steven."

"Hello, Mother."

Douglas Owen is a writer, author, editor, and publisher. He spends the majority of time behind a computer editing books and stories for his publishing company, DAOwen Publications.

Doug started the writing journey when his interests in adventure games lead him to create many different scenarios for his friends. Later in life he found himself writing training manuals, and teaching two cats how to sit up for dinner.

His interest in reading took him on a roundabout tour of short stories and flash fiction until one friend told him to just write a book. His first work still holds a special place in his heart, but he started publishing with The Spear series. All four YA fiction books were written during NaNoWriMo.

Doug continues to write whenever possible. His fiction can be found online and in many publications.

In 2013, Doug started writing for Self-Publisher Magazine. His entertaining and engrossing series, A Written View, engages new and seasoned writers with advice and information on the writing and publishing world. When the magazine turned into Indyfest Magazine, Doug took over the circulation.

Late in 2015, Doug opened DAOwen Publications and started taking submission. His fingers have been sore ever since.

Doug resides in Goodwood Ontario where he lives with his wife and three well loved cats.